Spare Me

VINNY MINCHILLO

Cover design and illustration by Jonathan Rice, www.jriceco.com

Visit the bowling center at www.SpareMeBook.com

This is a work of fiction. Names, characters, businesses, places, events, bowling ball names and incidents are either the products of the author's imagination or used in a fictitious manner. Any resemblance to actual persons, living or dead, or actual events is purely coincidental.

Yo Vinny Productions
Plano, Texas

ISBN: 0692451943
ISBN-13: 978-0692451946

To Barbara

For your patience, for your humor and for making sure I came back went I went too far.

ACKNOWLEDGMENTS

Thanks to everyone who sat through hours of bowling questions, listened to bad bowling jokes, proofread, edited, ran to get bowling pins (vital to the writing process), lent me bowling balls and shared their knowledge. Especially thanks to my family and double especially to my wife, Barbara, and daughter, Natalie, who were involuntarily roped into this adventure, but worked on it with incredible energy and enthusiasm.

And thank you to America's bowlers. Good, honest people who truly love their game.

1

TWO KNOCKS. SHORT AND HARD. Louie the Tongue knew what those knocks meant and he was ready. His affairs were in order and the best he could hope for now was a nice turnout at the funeral. But he wasn't ready for what he saw in the yellow glow of his porch light.

"What the hell is this?," Louie the Tongue asked. "Who are you?"

"I work for Uncle Sally."

"The nephew, right? Little Sally?"

"Yes," he sighed.

"Did I miss something? Is it fucking trainee day?"

"What?"

Louie leaned out of his front door to look behind the pudgy figure of Sally.

"Did your mother drop you off? Jesus Christ, Little Sally, I don't even get the respect of a real hit man to knock me off? Madone!"

"C'mon Louie, don't make this any harder than it

has to be."

"Why don't you run along and play cops and robbers on somebody else's porch."

Little Sally had to think fast. What would a real hit man do in this situation? Sally had never really punched anyone before, so he sort of threw his meaty fist toward Louie's face, grabbed him by the shirt and dragged him out to the car. Too bad it didn't shut him up. Now he knew why they called him the Tongue.

"Ow, you punched me in the nose, you fat fuck."

Sally was ready to kill this guy right here on the sidewalk.

"Wait a minute, is that your car?," Louie said holding his nose as blood poured onto his shirt. "You gotta be shitting me. A goddamn Chevy Cavalier, what about respect? I did a lot of good things for this family. You can't haul me away in a Caddy, at least a Lincoln?"

"Get in the car."

Sally pulled open the door with the intent of shoving Louie in the back seat. Couple of problems. For starters, the Cavalier was a two-door compact, so he was going to have to tilt the seat forward and shove Louie in headfirst. Before he could tilt the seat forward he had to get Old Frank out.

"Oh for Christ's sake," Louie started up again. "You brought Old Frank? You and Old Frank? They couldn't find a couple of Girl Scouts? What the fuck, Frank, we go way back."

Back in the day, Old Frank wasn't Old Frank. He was Big Bang Frank, one of the baddest, most feared men alive. He didn't kill you with a nice, clean .22 behind the ear. When Frank came calling, you got the Big Bang. Frank did the bad jobs. The rats, the killers, the flippers, the people who needed to be sent out with a certain type of message. The kind of message that told others, don't even think about doing what this guy did.

A few of his greatest hits included impaling a guy on the tail fin of his Cadillac, doing a variation of cement shoes called the cement hat and, when you hear about some mook getting shoved into a wood chipper, say a little thank you to Big Bang Frank.

Unfortunately, the years had not been kind to Frank. Call it dementia, Alzheimer's or just karma, Frank lost his marbles. He still had a few moments of clarity, but mostly he just sat in a chair and giggled watching Fox News. For some reason, Hannity cracked him up.

Louie took one more shot. "C'mon, Old Frank, for old times' sake."

"Sally brought me some Pringles, but they were the wrong kind," Old Frank said.

Sally thought, I might shoot both of these guys. Or maybe I'll shoot myself first.

Too bad he only brought one bullet.

Since birth, Salvatore Cusamano, Jr. had been called Little Sally. He hated that nickname. Every Italian family had a Sally. And if there were two Sallies, one was Big Sally and one was Little Sally. If you were Little Sally, you were destined for a hard life on the elementary school playground. But today was the last time anyone would call him Little Sally. From now on, he would be known as One Bullet.

Yeah, One Bullet, that was a nickname Little Sally

could live with. He would be a legend, be feared, be respected. He would set the bar higher than any hit man before or after. He would do the deal with just one bullet. Not only would he kill them with a single shot, he wouldn't even bother bringing a second bullet.

He'd be like the Man With The Golden Gun. Only Italian. With asthma.

Trouble was, Little Sally didn't have one bullet or a gun to shoot it with. So he went where he always went when he needed something – Wal-Mart. Which is how he wound up with a camouflage-painted Remington 870 shotgun (that came with a free pair of matching camouflage sweatpants) and a box of Buckhammer slugs. Sally slipped one slug into his pocket, tossed the Remington in the trunk and he was on the road to hit man stardom.

Little Sally got Old Frank out of the front seat, jammed Louie the Tongue in the back, ran down the street to catch Old Frank who had wandered off, shoved Louie back into the car, got Old Frank in, found his Pringles and finally got the hell out of there. If he hung around much longer he might as well join the homeowner's association.

Louie was quiet. For about 30 seconds.

"Be honest with me Sally, have you ever whacked anybody before?"

"Sure, lots of times."

"Don't lie to me, Sally, don't lie to a dead man."

"He's a first timer," Old Frank said, picking a bad time to be lucid.

"Thanks, Old Frank," Sally said, a little too late.

"Holy fuck," screamed the Tongue. "I'm gonna get whacked by a first timer. You got a bullet with training wheels? Oh look, here's a copy of 'Assassination for Dummies.' I can not fucking believe this."

"Louie," Sally said, "don't make me stop this car."

When they turned into the landfill things got even worse.

"You're going to dump my body in a landfill? That's cold. What did I do to deserve this?"

Sally dragged Louie out of the Cavalier's back seat, grabbed Old Frank before he could get away again and locked him in the car.

"Jesus H. Christ," Louie shook his head.

Then Sally pulled out the Remington.

"Okay, seriously, do I really deserve to be thrown into a garbage dump after I get shot by a trainee with a, what the hell, is that a camouflage shotgun? I can't believe that I don't..."

Sally pulled out the shell and held it up.

"Louie, I got one bullet with your name on it. That's why they call me – One Bullet."

"Listen, you don't want to do this...One Bullet? What the fuck is that supposed to mean?"

"It's only gonna take one bullet to kill you, so that's all I brought."

"Really? That was the best idea you had?"

The sound of Sally racking a round into the Remington finally shut the Tongue up. At least it would have if Sally didn't drop the shell trying to load it.

"Aw shit."

Sally dropped down on his knees in the darkness

and started pawing through the dirt to try to find the shell.

"Take your time, douche bag, I got all night."

"Hang on a second."

"It's next to your left foot, jackass."

"Oh, thanks."

Sally jammed the shell in the gun and racked it home.

"Just make it so my wife can have a nice funeral, okay?"

"As long as you're dead and quiet, she'll probably have a really nice day."

A 12-gauge shotgun firing a slug sounds like an explosion. Inside your skull. Your ears ring, your head pounds and the gun tries to rip itself out of your hands. And when you hit someone with a 12-gauge slug? Suffice to say you won't need to fire it again. Depending on where you aim.

"You stupid son of a bitch! You fucking missed?"

Sally fired the shotgun from the hip. It was a shotgun, how much aiming was really required? Quite a bit it turns out. Sally caught Louie in the shoulder which, for some reason, made him talk even more.

"C'mon, you dumb bastard, finish me off. Pump the shotgun and finish me off."

"I can't."

"What?"

"I only brought the one bullet. I don't have any more bullets."

"Oh my God, the idiot didn't bring any bullets. To a hit. So instead of being killed like a man, I'm just going to bleed to death at the landfill. This is fucking perfect."

Sally started rummaging around the trunk in the

hopes of finding another shotgun shell in there. Wal-Mart bag? No shells. Bowling bag? No ball. No baseball bat. No tire iron. The only thing of any size he could lay his paws on was his mother's Crock Pot that he was supposed to be bringing back from his Aunt Rose's house. If anything happened to that Crock Pot his mother would kill him, but Sally was going to have to use it to kill someone else first.

With the first swing he brought the pot straight down on top of Louie's head producing a loud scream and a groan. The second swing finally shut Louie up. Swings three through 15 finished him off. The Crock Pot wasn't looking too good, either.

As far as Sally was concerned, he was born and bred to be a ruthless killing machine. That was his calling. Of course, his parents, Mr. and Mrs. Cusamano, pegged him as more of a tax attorney or a dermatologist. Mrs. Cusamano wasn't a big fan of her brother's business. Gambling, booze, drugs. Surrounds himself with thugs. Maybe he had done some really bad things, maybe he hadn't, she didn't want to know, but he bought their mother a house so now he's practically a saint. She named her son after Sally because her mother guilted her into it. Now the kid thinks he's a hit man. Jesus Christ, how could I be such a pushover, she thought, as she stubbed out her Kent cigarette in the remnants of a slice of Entenmann's coffee cake.

Little Sally didn't care much for tax law or dermatology. He was a straight A student (zero absences from kindergarten through twelfth grade, by the way) and could have waltzed into either law school or medical school. Instead, as his mother would tell you, he set out to crush the hopes and dreams she had for her only son.

"How many hit men do you know who have asthma?," his mother said, trying anything to get her Little Sally to see the light.

"No problem, Ma, I'll take my inhaler with me."

"And how will that work, Mr. Smarty Pants Hit Man? Hang on a second, I'm going to kill you as soon as I find my inhaler and catch my breath."

"Oh Ma."

"Don't 'Oh, Ma' me. Hit men spend all their time in damp, cold places like landfills and marshes digging shallow graves and dragging bodies around late at night. Not exactly an occupation for someone with breathing problems and a sensitivity to rashes. Not to mention the mosquitos."

She had a point. And she seemed to know an awful lot about what hit men did.

But Little Sally had a goal.

To make sure no one ever called him Little Sally ever again.

So Little Sally ignored his mother and begged Uncle Sally to let him start doing odd jobs. Pick ups, deliveries, get the Cadillac washed, drive a car with New York license plates to North Carolina and drive a very similar car with North Carolina plates back. Uncle Sally had high hopes for Little Sally. He was a big kid, smart, did what he was told. Uncle Sally never had a son, maybe this kid could be a decent substitute.

The trouble was Little Sally wasn't cut out for the life. He didn't like to drink, didn't like to fight, didn't like to stay up late and, worst of all, Little Sally really liked to bowl. He carried an impressive 180 average, not that anyone noticed. Or cared.

Hit men didn't bowl.

Even if the family business headquarters was inside a bowling alley.

"For chrissakes, Little Sally," Uncle Sally would yell at him. "Put down that goddamn bowling ball and do some work."

Little Sally was prepared to do whatever it took to become a hit man. Including telling anybody and everybody he thought could help him. Little Sally was the least discreet hit man wannabe the world had ever known.

"Need anybody rubbed out today, Uncle Sally?," he'd ask.

"No one has said that since 1947," Uncle Sally replied. "Here, go wash the Caddy. And don't let them spray any of that spring flower air freshener crap in my car. Last time my Cadillac smelled like an old French whore."

Becoming a hit man was only half the dream. The big picture was that hit men didn't really work that often, short periods of intense activity and then long stretches of time off. The perfect way to pay the bills to fund his life on the pro bowling tour. While other kids kept Playboy magazines under their mattresses, Little Sally stashed copies of Bowling Digest under his.

"Snap out of it, you idiot," Uncle Sally said. "Listen. Big Mike tore his trapezio acidophilus muscle or some shit like that. I need you to step in."

Big Mike was the muscle of the family. A simple man who enjoyed lifting weights, shooting steroids and crushing skulls with baseball bats. He wasn't a big thinker, but he was a pretty valuable part of the family and had very little interest in letting some schmuck like Little Sally horn in on the action. Of course, Big Mike was a realist, if he didn't make it look like he was playing nice with the boss' nephew he might find himself welded into a 55-gallon drum. Still, that didn't mean he had to make things easy.

But that's exactly what he did.

Big Mike was in the gym, as usual, wearing one of those thick, leather weightlifting belts and carrying a gallon milk jug filled with steroid-charged water. He grunted with every lift and threw down the weight bar with a flourish. And nobody complained. The last guy who did wound up with a broken sternum and a gallon of water poured over his head. Big Mike wasn't exactly Mr. Personality, but he did have a way with people.

Trying to max out for a new personal best, Big Mike was dead lifting enough weight to crush a Hyundai when he heard something pop in his shoulder. To avoid further injury he opened his hands and let the weight bar drop. Right on his pinkie toe. As he sank to the floor he thought, that little bastard Sally is going to get my hit. He looked down to see his Nike filling up with blood and laughed knowing that the boss would make him take Old Frank along since it was Little Sally's first hit. He almost felt sorry for him.

"Okay," Uncle Sally said, "with Big Mike hurt, you and Old Frank need to take care of a little problem I have."

Little Sally sighed to himself. Or he thought it was to himself.

"You got a fucking problem with Old Frank? Listen, someday you're gonna be old and senile and not remember if you put your prick back in your pants after you've taken a leak."

Old Frank was sitting about three feet away during all this, laughing to himself. What he was laughing at no one was really sure.

"Either you take Old Frank or I freelance this out."

"No, no. I love Old Frank, it'll be great. Right Old Frank?"

"Pringles!," came the reply.

Even though Sally beat Louie to death with a small kitchen appliance, wrapped up his body and threw it in a pit all by himself, he knew one thing for sure. His One Bullet story was going to stick. No one was going to know what really happened, so he could tell it any way he wanted. Old Frank doesn't even know if he's wearing pants, let alone what happened at the landfill.

Next day at the bowling alley, Sally was ready to tell the tale.

"How'd it go?," Uncle Sally asked.

"Louie nearly talked me to death."

"You let Louie talk?," said Big Mike, wearing an arm sling and a boot guarding his rebuilt pinkie toe. "You're such a pussy."

"Shut up."

"I'll fucking kill you," Mike hissed.

"Take it easy, boys," Uncle Sally said.

Mike limped out of the room, but managed to lean over to Sally and whispered, "I mean, I'll fucking kill you as soon as I get the chance."

"How'd it go, Old Frank? How'd the boy do?," said Uncle Sally.

"He shot him and missed. Then no more bullets. So he beats the guy to death with a fucking Crock-Pot. Funniest thing I've ever seen," Old Frank recalled.

"Old Frank, you're too funny," Sally laughed nervously. "I shot him with one bullet. One. Bullet. In fact, I only brought...one...bullet."

"And the Pringles," said Uncle Frank.

"Looks like you're a real tough guy now," Uncle Sally said.

The heavens opened. This was the moment Little Sally had been waiting for his whole life. The head of a major crime family had given him his first hit job and was about to bestow upon him the nickname that would cement his reputation as a tough guy and launch his career.

"Nice going, Crock Pot."

2

RAY FLANAGAN HAD TO TAKE A WICKED LEAK.

Generally speaking, Ray didn't get along very well with his internal organs. And right now, his prostate was really hacking him off.

Or as Ray called it, his "prostrate."

Damn prostrate, he said to himself, it's the size of a friggin' Subaru.

Having something the size of a sensible Japanese car pressing on his bladder meant Ray Flanagan had to pee in a major, Russian racehorse kind of way. And since his Ford F450 delivery truck did not come factory equipped with a urinal and the Bronx's Major Deegan Expressway had exactly zero rest areas, he had a serious problem. But Ray was nothing if not a problem solver. He punched the button on the glovebox and yanked out a tortured coat hanger wrapped around a length of garden hose with a funnel jammed into the end. Steering with his knee, a technique expressly forbidden by the New York State commercial driving code and perfected by Ray after years of dedicated practice, he fed the pre-bent wire over the steering column and slipped the garden hose through a rusty hole in the floorboard. The wire positioned the funnel at crotch height. Ray, not a big believer in seat belts anyway, preferring instead to be thrown clear of the wreckage in case of a big accident, wiggled up to the edge of the seat, opened his fly and let nature take its course.

He glanced up just in time to see the Buick behind him switch on the windshield wipers. Seemed odd, the woman behind the wheel thought, for it to rain on a perfectly clear day. A sun shower, she supposed. Ray looked in the rear view and smiled. Something Ray didn't do much anymore.

With a little extra room in the pipes, he reached into the pocket of his old plaid hunting jacket and slipped out the second Old Milwaukee tall boy he had picked up at lunch. You see, Ray was what used to be called a drinker. These days he qualified for any number of insurance-approved psychological maladies, but he didn't need any therapy or medications, alcohol helped him cope fine. Ray wasn't an alcoholic, he just liked to drink, there's a difference.

Except recently his lifelong drinking partner had turned on him. After fifty years of dutifully straining booze out of his blood, his liver decided to call it quits. Ungrateful bag of goo. Call something a vital organ and it gets all uppity. Ray's liver wasn't the only problem, there was a lot of this quitting bullshit going around lately.

His wife quit six months ago. They had been together ever since he felt her up in the back seat of his Dad's Oldsmobile. In fact, that was the high point of their 43-year relationship. It wasn't a big surprise that she left, Ray just thought the whole thing would have played out more like on TV. He figured she would shack up with a tennis instructor or a muscle-bound pool boy. Never mind the fact that they didn't have a pool and she never played a game of tennis in her life. Ray's wife left for one simple reason: she was sick of Ray. Nothing in particular. It wasn't the drinking or the distance or the arguing or the boredom or the unfulfilled dreams or the wasted years. She was just sick of looking at his face every day, so she packed up and left. Ray figured it was better than her going full-on lesbo, but not much.

Fine, he'd get along without her. He knew how to get to the grocery store, he could probably figure out the microwave and he had a brand new package of Jockey underwear ready to go. (Ray had always been a Hanes man, but after seeing the commercials a few years ago where Michael Jordan insisted on wearing a Hitler mustache, he made the switch.) What else did a man need? Ray could watch what he wanted to watch, eat what he wanted to eat and bowl whenever he wanted to bowl. Damn, he missed her sometimes, but he knew he'd be okay without her.

Ray couldn't say the same thing about his liver. He had half a mind to reach down his own throat and punch that good-for-nothing thing right in the bile duct. His liver was a quitter and Ray hated quitters. But then again, how hard was it to put a new liver into somebody these days? Ray read the papers, it seemed like every week some creaky old movie star was pickling his liver in 18-year-old scotch only to have a crack team of doctors at Cedars-Sinai jam in a new one like they were putting a water pump into an old Chevy pickup. Two weeks later the guy's crying on Dr. Oz.

The doctors working on Ray's case sprung into

action just like on TV. Unfortunately, they were all working to find a new heart for a Hall of Fame pitcher who collapsed in a strip club while his wife was across town undergoing chemotherapy. The public outpouring of support was touching. The last time Ray saw his doctor was on TV during the press conference celebrating the successful transplant. All Ray got was a battered manila envelope filled with complicated forms and bad Xerox copies of brochures with titles like "Me And My Cirrhosis" and "I Need A New Liver, Now What?"

The manila envelope slowly gave up its secrets, including the existence of "the list" of who got a liver next. Ugh, a list, Ray thought. That meant filling out forms in triplicate and, of course, a phone call with a bureaucrat who has one eye on a ham sandwich and the other eye on the clock.

"Name?," said the disinterested voice on the other end of the line at the VA.

"Flanagan, Ray."

"Organ requiring transplantation?"

"Liver, but if you come across a nice looking spleen I'd be interested in that, too."

"Spleen, sir?"

"Just joking."

"I see."

The old Ray Flanagan charm wasn't working.

"Do you use tobacco?"

"Nope."

Ray smoked about a pack, pack and a half a day, but he didn't chew tobacco, that was disgusting.

"Do you use alcohol?"

"What do you mean by use?"

"Drink alcohol, sir, do you drink?"

Ray was good for a six-pack of tall boys a night, he'd blow through a couple of cases on a weekend during football season. As far as Ray was concerned, that wasn't drinking and beer wasn't alcohol. Alcohol came in bottles.

"Occasionally," Ray answered.

"About how much do you drink?"

"Maybe a mixed drink or two on special occasions." Ray defining special occasions as things like Saturdays.

"Beer or wine?"

"Beer counts as alcohol?"

"Yes, sir," she said between bites of a sandwich. "How much beer do you drink?"

"Maybe a beer or three in the evening, a few more on bowling nights." Ray wondered what difference it made. The liver he had was shot anyway.

"Sir, if a new liver is transplanted into you, you'll have to give up alcohol completely."

Ray's gast was flabbered. The whole point of getting a new liver was to get Ray back into prime drinking form. Beer was about the only thing that hadn't quit on Ray and now this government hack was telling him he'd have to give up drinking to get one?

"Wait a minute. Completely?"

"Yes, sir."

"I'm certainly willing to give up hard liquor, it's expensive anyway."

"All alcohol, sir."

"Beer?"

"Yes."

"Ale?"

"Yes."

"Malt liquor?"

"Yes."

"Wine coolers?"

"Yes."

"Jagermeister?"

"Yes."

"That was a trick question, nobody drinks Jagermeister except on their 21st birthday."

No response.

"Can I have a little glass of sherry if I promise to drink it with my pinkie sticking out?"

"No alcohol at all, sir."

This was going to be rough.

"Sir, let's talk about your lifestyle."

It just got rougher.

"Married?"

"Divorced, but it turns out she's not a lesbian," Ray helpfully pointed out.

"How active are you?"

"I don't lay in bed all day. I get up and go drive a truck."

"Do you exercise?"

"Yes, I go bowling."

"I meant, real exercise, like jogging or weight lifting."

"Bowling isn't real exercise? And weight lifting? My bowling ball is 16 pounds." She hit a sore spot with Ray. "You know, bowling's on the verge of being in the Olympics."

"Curling is in the Olympics, sir."

"Another fine sport where having a beer in your hand doesn't hurt your chances for victory."

She checked the box marked "sedentary."

Ray was pretty well at the end of his rope now.

"Here's a question," he said, "what if I were to get my own liver?"

"I'm sorry, sir?"

"Let's just say, hypothetically, that I came into possession of a liver, you guys could put it in, right? Like if I brought an alternator to a mechanic and they would put it in for me."

"Well, sir, I don't know if..."

"Just between you and me, okay? Say I go out and find a guy about my size, we want to make sure his liver's gonna fit right the first time, and I hit him in the head with a shovel. I have to be careful not to hit him too hard, I don't want to kill him, I just want to put him into a really deep coma. At that point, should I call you guys to come get him or should I just toss him in the back of my truck and bring us both in at the same time?"

"Sir, that's not how it..."

"I've got my eye on one guy in particular. Does it matter if he drinks and bowls?"

"I'm going to have to switch you to my manager."

"Take it easy, I'm just kidding with you. So how long until I get a liver? Week or two? I'd like to wait until after the next bowling tournament if that's possible."

"You'll hear from one of our counselors in the next six to eight weeks, sir."

"Will they just deliver the new liver to the doctor's office?"

"Something like that, sir."

"In the meantime, what kind of shovel would you recommend?"

"I'm sorry?"

"You know, to put the guy in a coma. A garden

spade or a square shovel? I thought about a snow shovel, but I don't think that would really work."

"Sir, I don't think that's a good idea."

"You're right. Let's go with the garden spade."

Click.

3

IT'S NO PICNIC being in a serious relationship with a professional athlete.

That's what Leonard Fleischman told himself as his girlfriend slammed the door in his face.

Not coincidentally, it's also what he told her right before she slammed the door in his face.

"It's no picnic being in a serious relationship with a professional athlete?," she said. "If I ever get into a relationship with a professional athlete, I'll let you know how it goes."

"Wait a minute," Leonard said, "you are in a relationship with a professional athlete. Me."

"You're not an athlete, Leonard. You're a bowler. With no future."

"I thought you were going to start calling me Bud like everyone else does?"

"No one calls you Bud, Leonard, and you need to give this up. A professional athlete doesn't unclog toilets and spray disinfectant into rented shoes."

"Look, I'm just paying my dues for a little while, as soon as I get on the tour..."

"You mean the tour where you travel for weeks at a time bowling for a chance to win dozens of dollars? Then right back to your job unclogging toilets."

"I'm the head pro at Massapequa Pin and Pub."

"You're the head nobody, Leonard. I can't stake my future on a man who fixes shoelaces all day."

"Is that what you think I do?"

"Yes."

"For your information, maintaining the rental shoes is just a small part of my job."

"Listen Leonard, you're a wonderful guy. For somebody. Just not me."

"I know you're upset. Don't worry, I'm willing to take you back."

"I'm not coming back, Leonard."

"I'll never stop loving you."

"Please, Leonard."

"Even when I'm on TV accepting one of those giant checks, I'll be thinking of you."

"Goodbye Leonard."

When the love of your life slams the door in your face, it's tough to knock on that door again. But Leonard had a question that could not go unasked.

"Um," he said, when she opened the door. "Can I have my 300 ring back?"

"300 rings?"

"No, my 300 ring, the one I got when I bowled my first perfect game. Remember, I gave it to you to wear on a chain around your neck?"

"Right, right. Kind of looks like a high school class ring?"

"No, it looks like a Super Bowl ring, just scaled down a little. You know, it's one of the highest honors in our sport, because it represents the perfect game, which is 12 strikes in a row. Those 300 rings are awarded by the American Bowling Congress and they're pretty rare."

Unless you look on eBay and have an extra 50 bucks burning a hole in your PayPal account.

Most of Leonard's lecture was delivered to an empty door frame. He could hear her rummaging through that drawer everyone has in their kitchen filled with rubber bands, batteries, half-empty tubes of glue, extra house keys and perfect 300 game bowling rings.

"Is this it?"

There it was. Leonard's highest achievement in the world of sports glittering in 10 karat gold plate with a synthetic garnet stone, authentic diamond chips and a piece of sweater fuzz hanging off the second zero in 300.

"Thanks. It means a lot to me."

Leonard had been playing the scene over and over in his head until the bowling center manager snapped him out of it. As the resident pro, Leonard was often summoned to help a player struggling with their game. Would it be an issue with the bowler's swing?, he wondered. Maybe footwork. Or perhaps the toughest of all, a mental block preventing the bowler from reaching their true potential as an athlete.

"Leonard! The men's room toilet is clogged again," Al shouted.

"C'mon, Al, I've told you a hundred times to call me Bud."

"Whatever Leonard, just unclog the crapper."

"I'm the resident pro here, why don't we hire a maintenance man to take care of things like this?"

"Then what would you do?"

"Excuse me? I give lessons, consult on bowling ball selections, custom drill the balls, give advice to help our customers become better bowlers."

"Then you better go over and talk to that birthday party of eight-year-olds. Little Suzy there has put 22 in a row right in the gutter. Tell her it's all in the wrist."

Al DiMateo was what some people might call, an asshole. Trouble is, that term implies the person involved was putting forth some kind of effort to be something at all. Al DiMateo wasn't about to do anything for any reason, which made him the perfect man for the job.

Being the manager of Massapequa Pin and Pub required a certain kind of business acumen. Specifically, a bad one. Al's job was brutally simple: make sure the Pin and Pub lost money. And plenty of it.

Massapequa Pin and Pub, founded in 1957, billed itself as a family fun center, arcade, sports bar, lounge, party place, corporate outing destination and Long Island's Official Bar and Bat Mitzvah Headquarters. No one was sure if there was an organization that regularly bestowed that particular honor on different establishments, but Al thought it sounded good in the brochure.

The trick was to spend enough money to look like it was successful, but on paper make sure the place was losing a fortune. If the bowling alley bought bowling pins for fifteen dollars a piece, Al put them in the books for a hundred dollars a pop. Turning 10 dollars in cash into 90 dollars worth of nice, clean, government-issued tax write-offs, something actually worth more than cash to the boss. Sure, adding all those zeroes was hard work, but Al was up to the task. As long as he didn't have to get out of his chair to do it.

Al was good at losing money. On the horses, on football, on ex-wives. Which was how Al wound up working for dear old Uncle Sally in the first place.

Uncle Sally was the generous type who was quick with the checkbook when it came to local charities. Especially the local charities that would get Uncle Sally's picture in the paper holding a plaque.

Does your little league team need uniforms? Call Uncle Sally. Lost your job and can't afford a wheelchair for your disabled son? Call Uncle Sally. Need to have somebody's balls cut off because they cheated on your sister? Uncle Sally could handle that, too.

You see, Uncle Sally was in the business.

Everyone knew Uncle Sally was also Salvatore DeNuccio, head of one of Long Island's biggest crime families. Granted, that's like being the tallest of short men, but Sal had built himself a real nice business doing all the usual stuff. Running numbers, protection, prostitution, contract fixing, a little bit of drugs here and there, nothing too crazy. Trouble was, a business like Uncle Sally's came with a unique problem. Too much cash and not enough reasons to have it.

That's when he came up with the two simple words that changed everything: Bowling. Alley.

"I want to buy a bowling alley, Morty."

"Nobody bowls, Sally," his accountant, Morty Rubenstein, an expert at keeping two and three sets of books, told him.

"I know that, Morty," Sally said.

"Why don't you just punch yourself in the face? Bowling is dying."

"I know that, too, Morty."

"If you buy a bowling alley you're going to lose a fortune."

"Exactly, Morty."

"Ah. Oh. You! You're something else, Sally."

"Buy it. Whatever they want, plus 10 percent."

"Cash?"

"Cash."

And so it began. When the first mob family showed how easy it was to lose money in the bowling business, the rest of them couldn't jump in fast enough. The Calabreses bought Smithtown 300. The Marchiondas picked up the Wantagh Fun Center. The Magnani Brothers squeezed out the owners of the Center Moriches Bowlarama (earning the brothers the nickname the Sons of Bitches from Center Moriches). And the McElwaines (half-Italian on their mother's side) ran the Baldwin Big Bonanza of Bowling.

It was a beautiful thing. A bowling alley had everything an enterprising organized crime boss could ever want. A legitimate front of a business, a bar with a real live liquor license, plenty of storage, lots of parking, no-questions-asked 24-hour operation and a bottomless pit to throw cash into.

Cash goes in, write-offs come out.

Massapequa Pin and Pub was the model and it ran like a well-oiled money-losing machine.

Until the Zamboni crashed through the wall.

And the gunfire started.

4

BY 1949, FRANK ZAMBONI had perfected the ice resurfacing machine that would bear his name, inspire songs and fascinate generations of hockey fans. Built on the chassis of surplus military jeeps, the four wheel drive Zamboni machines were tough and durable. And some said they still had a little fight left in them.

That certainly applied to the Zamboni that appeared where the wall used to be.

Zamboni machines did not belong in bowling alleys, but Massapequa Pin and Pub had one stuck in the gutters between lanes 29 and 30.

One quick look at the machine revealed that it was from Sergei's House of Ice and All-Night Lounge (billed as "Your one stop shop for all your hockey, figure skating, birthday party and drinking needs") located next door to the Pin and Pub.

Sergei was not what you would call a good neighbor. A former third string goalie with the minor league Long Island Ducks hockey team and the first goalie to be suspended for instigating three fights in two games, Sergei and his family operated a slightly illegal side business out of the hockey rink. Over time, Sergei and Uncle Sally had formed an uneasy truce.

"Look, you can run all the drugs you want," Uncle

Sally told him, "I don't like messing with that crap, but you keep your nose out of the numbers and the girls."

"Fuck you," Sergei offered.

Sergei was horning in on Uncle Sally's hard won territory. Something would have to be done about Sergei, but Uncle Sally hadn't gotten around to formulating a plan.

In the meantime, Sergei found his own plan. Somewhere near the bottom of a bottle of Stoli.

"Fuck that stupid old Italian," Sergei said. "Let's just get rid of him and take over the bowling alley, too."

It sounded very menacing in Sergei's Russian accent coming out of his disfigured face covered with the railroad tracks of over 300 stitches.

"We do it today," he screamed. "Right now."

In the middle of an afternoon figure skating lesson, Sergei, his brother Ivan and their friend Guy, a French Canadian former hockey teammate, grabbed up three AK-47s, a bunch of ammunition, a fresh bottle of vodka and climbed aboard the Zamboni.

Guy, being French Canadian, was the only one who knew how to drive the Zamboni. He never took a lesson or anything, it's just something French Canadians know how to do instinctively.

"We go straight srough zee wall," Guy yelled in a thick French accent over the drone of the Zamboni engine.

"What is he saying?," Sergei shouted.

"I can never understand a word he says with that stupid accent," Ivan said back.

With that, Guy gunned the Zamboni engine, ran it up to its top speed of nine miles an hour and aimed for the other end of the ice rink. A twirling figure skater barely spun out of the way. A 13-year-old boy dropped his sister from high overhead causing her to shatter her ankle and their Olympic dreams. Any number of salchows and toe loops and spinning camels were ruined in mid-execution.

The heavy duty Zamboni flattened the ice rink boards and slammed hard into the concrete cinder block wall. Between the shoddy workmanship, substandard building materials and watered down mortar provided by a friend of Uncle Sally's who may or may not have been skimming a little off the top, the wall dropped down like a Lego set on Christmas morning.

The Zamboni came to rest teetering across the last two lanes of the bowling alley with the engine screaming at full throttle and all four wheels spinning in the air. And Sergei standing on the hood with a fully loaded AK and a head full of vodka.

Big Mike was the first one out of the back office. Even with his left arm in a sling from the torn trapezius muscle and his right foot in a compression boot, he was still the fastest guy on the team. He peeked around the corner in time to see Sergei unload the first clip of the machine gun.

A stream of bullet holes started to appear around the walls of Massapequa Pin and Pub. The Ladies' Day Bowling League, a thinly veiled cover for daytime drinking, hit the floor in unison. They gasped as the bullets shattered three rows of liquor bottles behind the bar.

No one was more upset than full-time barfly and part-time Nassau County police detective Tommy Hanrahan. A NATO round zinged right over his head and shattered a bottle of 18-year-old Glenlivet single malt scotch. That was a serious offense.

Al, born and raised a coward, was hiding under the bar.

"Hey Tommy," he said. "Maybe you should do something about this, you're a cop, ain't ya?"

"I'm not a cop, I'm a detective. Maybe if he leaves some fingerprints I'll get right on it."

"Don't you have a gun?"

"Of course, I have a gun."

"Does it have any bullets?"

"Don't know, never checked."

Hanrahan was 19 years toward a 20-year pension and two scotch and sodas closer to a nice afternoon buzz. And now that Russian jackass was shooting up the bowling alley. Sure, part of him knew he should do something about it, but a much bigger part of him wanted to make it to retirement. Taking on the Russian mob in a gunfight was not going to get him any closer to a cabin in the Adirondacks.

Tommy had a good thing going. He drew a nice little paycheck from the county on the first and fifteenth, had dental insurance and, as long as he cracked a case once in a while, the boss stayed off his ass. Then there was Tommy's second job, a little security work at the bowling alley. Mostly securing a little higher blood alcohol level.

His job was simple. Keep the cops out of the bowling alley and tip off Uncle Sally if anything happened that could be bad for business. In exchange, Tommy got paid double his cop salary. In cash. And then every few months, Uncle Sally would throw him some low life dipshit to arrest so he could keep things copacetic with the brass.

A few more months and Tommy could turn in his badge and start drinking full time. He didn't need any trouble, so when the shooting started, Hanrahan executed his signature move. He slipped out the side door, got in his car and left. He'd come back when the shooting stopped.

As Sergei began emptying the second clip, Leonard walked out of the men's room, dripping plunger in hand. He saw the bullets rake around the room and looked on in horror as the front window of the pro shop shattered. The drilling machine exploded into pieces, the new collection of microfiber bowling shirts was torn to shreds and, horror of horrors, Leonard's autographed photo of left-handed bowling legend Earl Anthony now had a huge hole where Earl's head used to be.

Leonard was a guy with a pretty long fuse, but disrespecting the legend of the great Earl Anthony was over the line. That's when Leonard saw the Rosenberg bar mitzvah.

Sergei was firing an automatic weapon exactly the way you'd expect a lunatic with a half bottle of cheap vodka in him would. And after a few hundred hockey fights, he may or may not have had a lingering head injury.

Sergei jammed a fresh magazine into the AK-47, racked back the slide and drew a bead on a group of teenagers frozen with fear.

Leonard saw it all happen in that weird kind of slow motion known only to people who have survived war and car accidents. He could see the muscles in Sergei's arm flex as he started to squeeze the trigger.

He had to stop Sergei, but how was a portly

aspiring pro bowler with no weapon, no training and no plan supposed to go up against three machine gun wielding thugs on a Zamboni? No chance.

War heroes always say the same thing. When they performed the act of heroism that earned them the medal and saved the day, they didn't have a plan or even an idea. They just reacted and let nature take its course. Later, Leonard would tell the same story.

He reached over to the ball rack, picked up a 12-pounder and started his approach.

5

MAN HAS ALWAYS PURSUED PERFECTION.

In art. In music. In overpriced Japanese quasi-luxury cars. And for Bernie Steers of Waukesha, Wisconsin, perfection came in the form of a 12-pound orb.

Bernie was a bowling ball engineer. A man who worked in the dark arts of urethane covers and strangely shaped cores.

"People don't realize what goes into a bowling ball," Bernie started in one Thanksgiving. "There's some amazing science in there. Get me a pen and paper."

Nobody could clear a room like Bernie.

There are people who bowl and then there are people who dedicate their lives to knocking down ten pins. Most of the people who live, eat and breathe bowling are the bowlers themselves. People with big swings, strong arms or a God-given gift to put the ball in the right place at the right time. Some people can just smell how a lane is oiled and know how much spin to put on the ball to get it to hook in just right.

Bernie had none of those skills. In fact, he was barely an average bowler. He had no special gift, wasn't particularly strong, had very little endurance. His gift was between his ears. He was a bowling ball engineering genius.

"A bowling ball is a lot like planet Earth," Bernie would say. "The urethane cover is like the crust. It looks smooth from a distance, but up close it's bumpy, rough and unpredictable. And inside is where the real magic lives. Think about the magma inside. Magma!"

Anyone who didn't leave the Thanksgiving table fell asleep instantly. Chalk it up to the tryptophan. Or Bernie.

Bowling ball engineers fell into two categories. You had your cover guys and your core guys. The cover guys thought the core guys were tin foil hat wearing dilettantes and the core guys thought the cover guys were lightweights who wouldn't know a good design if they engraved it on a bowling pin and bashed them over the head with it.

Bernie was one of the rare engineers who could do both, but instead of being the star of the department, he was shunned by the cover and core guys alike. That's why Bernie worked alone, which was fine with him.

He loved his work. Designing, experimenting, scrapping it all and starting over from scratch. He didn't drink, didn't chase women and never strayed from his calling to create a better bowling ball. If he wasn't at his desk at the office, he was at his desk at home.

Except Bernie never came home last night.

Bernie's wife Lorraine was beside herself. She and Bernie had been married for 34 years and he'd never disappeared. Not even once.

She called the Waukesha police and they gave her the usual song and dance about not being able to take a missing persons report until the person was gone at least 24 hours, blah, blah, blah.

"I checked at the office and they said he didn't show up this morning, either," Lorraine said.

"Where does he work?," deadpanned the cop.

"He's a research engineer at Wisco Bowling."

"We're sending a detective right over."

To say Waukesha was a company town was putting it mildly. Wisco, the world leader in bowling equipment, put Waukesha on the map and Waukesha took good care of its hometown hero. The police department took this responsibility very seriously. It's pretty unusual for a small town cop shop to have a dedicated Corporate Espionage Unit, but the Waukesha CEU was one of the best in the world. As the saying around the office went, there are no secrets in bowling, just the stuff that hasn't been stolen yet. The Waukesha CEU wanted to make sure the Wisco secrets stayed that way.

Mitch Dixon had been on the CEU team for six years and he'd seen it all. Break-ins, wiretaps, computer hacks, double agents, hidden cameras, even moles buried deep inside Wisco. And 99 percent of the time the trouble could be traced back to the same place: Shreveport, Louisiana, home of Wisco's biggest competitor, Pinknockerz.

If Wisco was the dark suit and starched white shirt of the bowling world, Pinknockerz (their tagline was "Bowlerz with Ballz") was the backwards hat and pants hanging down below the butt troublemaker. Wisco fans felt Pinknockerz didn't treat the game with respect. And when you name your balls things like Repeat Offender and Bad Tattoo, it was hard to disagree.

Mitch grew up hating Pinknockerz with a burning passion. Communists, country hicks, thieves, cheats. That's what you were taught about Pinknockerz from birth.

From a young age, Waukesha children learned bowling way beyond the basics. Bowling was a letter sport starting in the seventh grade. Elementary schools regularly participated in "Dress As Your Favorite Bowling Legend Day." The good kids would dress up as the left-handed Earl Anthony, the bad kids favored the hotheaded Dick Weber and there were always a few random Don Carters and Chris Schenkels. It was a red-letter day on the school calendar every year.

The kids were also trained to be vigilant. The word Pinknockerz was on the same level as Nazi Spy or Communist Sympathizer.

"What would you say if someone from Pinknockerz offered you candy?," said the CEU officer who conducted seminars at elementary school assemblies.

"No thanks!," they replied in unison. Waukesha children were nothing if not polite.

Even bowlers were suspect. Needless to say, everybody in Waukesha was a bowler. And everybody rolled a Wisco ball. If you switched to a Pinknockerz, even if it improved your game, it could ruin your life. Any decent bowling team would kick you off, you'd get the evil eye from the guy in the pro shop and people would whisper behind your back. Best case scenario, you'd be regarded as the village idiot.

Waukesha didn't care much for Pinknockerz.

The corporate espionage was the stuff of legend. Over the years, people touring the Wisco headquarters were relieved of spy camera glasses, audio recording devices, video cameras in purses, implantable bugs and USB drives. One person who was asking a lot of questions about urethane chemistry was found with a mass spectrometer hidden in a secret compartment of a Rascal scooter.

Then there was the great scandal of 1992. Sally Ann Jacobsen, the fact that she had two first names should have been a dead giveaway, was uncovered as an Pinknockerz spy working inside Wisco. Not just working in Wisco, but serving as personal assistant to the vice president of research and development. Sally Ann worked at Wisco for 15 years, was named departmental employee of the month three times, bowled on the team every Tuesday night, she was even fully vested in her 401k.

All that time, Sally Ann Jacobsen had been a spy. Every Wisco secret that went across her desk also went across the copier and into her purse. When she went home, she would fax the documents to Shreveport and burn them in her fireplace. Her neighbors thought it was odd she had her fireplace going in July, but they figured she was cold natured. Some people are like that.

The fact is, she shipped many of Wisco's best ideas to Pinknockerz. And she would have kept getting away with it if a partially burned confidential research and development memo hadn't flown out of her chimney and landed on a CEU detective's front porch. That detective was Mitch Dixon's dad.

Now Mitch was sitting in Bernie Steers' living room and didn't like what he was hearing.

"Mrs. Steers, was Mr. Steers working on anything in particular that you knew of?"

"Bernie was always working on something. It was bowling balls 24 hours a day."

"Any change in his behavior recently? Weight loss? Stress."

"Yes, now that you mention it. I could always tell when Bernie was close to a breakthrough. He never really talked about it, but I could tell he was really close to something. It would wear on him, you know."

"Any idea what it might be?"

"I don't really know, but he was always talking about the perfect bowling ball."

"The perfect bowling ball?"

"A ball that would change the game. A ball that couldn't miss."

"Is that even possible?"

"Bernie thought so. But for him it was like an atom bomb. He appreciated the achievement, but he also understood the dangers. That's why I'm worried. He knew what would happen if technology like that, if it even existed, fell into the wrong hands."

Mitch's CEU brain was tingling. This wasn't good. He was going to have call in the big guns. The Wisco Security Team. Bad people with itchy trigger fingers and a loose sense of morals. He had no choice, the future of bowling could be on the line.

"Susie, say hello to Detective Dixon."

"Hi," Susie Steers said.

"We named her after Earl Anthony's wife, Susie."

"That's nice."

"Are you going out, dear?"

Susie just rolled her eyes and walked into the

kitchen.

"Susie goes to community college. She's changed her major a few times. I think she's taking Sociology. Or Anthropology, I forget. Bernie likes to joke that she's on the ten year plan."

Susie walked out the back door carrying her bag. A Pinknockerz ball hidden inside.

6

THERE WERE SO MANY STORIES, the reporters didn't know where to start.

There were so many bullet holes, the police didn't know where to start.

Even the medical examiner just stood there with his hands in his pockets.

"This is going to suck. Hard," the medical examiner said. "We're gonna need a mop for that guy."

340 bullet holes. Broken glass everywhere. One ruined bar mitzvah. One broken drilling machine. (The extremely collectible autographed photo of Earl Anthony was not mentioned.) Three bodies, one disfigured so badly no one could tell if it was a man or a woman. Or even a person at all.

And one very angry man in an ambulance.

Witness reports varied. Wildly.

A few things were clear. It was just a typical afternoon at the bowling alley. A few bowlers on a few lanes and a pretty rowdy bar mitzvah going on. Couple of regular drunks in the bar and a few shady characters in the back.

Some people thought it was a bomb going off or some kind of gas explosion. They saw the wall crumble. Then things got weird. A giant Zamboni started clambering over chunks of broken cement block until it got stuck in the gutters between the last two lanes. The wheels were still grinding away, but the Zamboni was stuck.

That's when the gunfire started.

One man jumped on top of the hood of the Zamboni and started shooting all over the place. Another guy started firing from the driver's seat. A third man ran around to the front of the machine and started shooting. A big man with one arm in a sling and his foot in some kind of orthopedic boot limped out of the back office and started shooting back. An old man came out of the office with a shotgun and started shooting and screaming.

"Where the hell is Hanrahan?," the old man shouted over the automatic gunfire.

The guy on the top of the Zamboni reloaded his gun and took aim at a group of children across the bowling alley.

No one noticed as the young man, reported variously as the guy who sprays the stuff in the shoes or the guy who unclogs the toilets, grabbed a beat up orange ball off the rack, took five steps toward the Zamboni, swung the ball back as far as it could go and rolled it toward the gunfire. (Of course, no one reported the awesome footwork of sliding his right foot perfectly behind his left.) The ball rolled fast, but looked like it was about six feet wide of the mark. Suddenly, the spinning ball caught and hooked a hard left turn into the next to last lane heading straight for the left leg of the man standing in front of the Zamboni.

His leg never stood a chance. The tibia and fibula

put up almost no resistance snapping clean in two driving the broken bones straight through the skin. Ivan went down screaming. That didn't mean he stopped shooting. As he fell, the rapidly emptying AK-47 rode up, the last bullet leaving the barrel just in time to catch Sergei above the bridge of the nose and popping the top of his head clean off.

That left Guy behind the wheel still firing. Uncle Sally may have been a little rusty, but shooting at a thug with a sawed-off 12-gauge is like riding a bike. Bang, bang, Uncle Sally put two right into the former defenseman's chest making a hole big enough to check the weather outside. The force blew him back against the gearshift knocking the Zamboni into a lower gear and giving it just enough traction to climb out of the gutter. And over Ivan.

Poor Ivan. He was scraped, shaved and, adding insult to injury, covered with a spray of steaming hot water. The forensic team would have to pour the contents of the Zamboni's water tank through a flour sifter to get all of Ivan's remains into a body bag. More of a Tupperware container really.

When the Zamboni's wheels hit the goo that represented what was left of Ivan, the tires started to spin sending the engine straight to redline. The motor gave up with a bang sending one of the pushrods through the block, through the hood and right into the eye of Big Mike.

"The images we are about to show are graphic," the TV anchorman said.

"Might want to get the kids out of the room," his perky co-host added.

"This scene from a local bowling alley where a gunfight broke out."

"A local man is being hailed as a hero when he used a bowling ball to stop three gunmen."

They cut to shots of Leonard showing the motion he used to throw the ball across the alley.

"Leonard Fleischman, the bowling pro at Massapequa Pin and Pub, used a hook to take out the gunmen. He claims it was a lucky shot," the anchorwoman said.

"That's pretty GOOD luck," the anchorman added and they both chuckled. "Of course, there was also this gruesome injury."

The TV showed shaky news camera footage of a guy with a huge chest, an arm sling and a long piece of metal sticking out of his right eye.

The story went viral. It ran on the nightly news. Got picked up by Buzzfeed. Inside Edition breathlessly praised Leonard as the Bombing Bowler. He even received a phone call from an assistant to the Vice President of the United States.

Leonard Fleischman was a hero. With a bowling ball.

Google searches for bowling went through the roof. That night you couldn't find an open lane anywhere in the country. Bowling was back. All because of a guy named Leonard.

That meant bowling tournaments would be bigger and better with more prize money. Leagues would fill up instantly. Birthday parties would schedule. Bowling alleys would start making piles of money and the Massapequa Pin and Pub would go from a money laundering machine to a money making machine, which would make Uncle Sally very, very angry. And when the rest of the Long Island crime families started making money at their bowling alleys they'd know to point the finger at that stupid fuck who works for Uncle Sally.

Leonard saw this as his chance to make his move to the big time. The guys in the back room saw things a little bit differently.

Uncle Sally posed with Leonard for the cameras. He liked being in the paper and on TV, but inside, he was not a happy man.

And Big Mike? It's hard to think about much when you have a pushrod sticking out of your eye. Big Mike thought of only one thing. Kill Leonard Fleischman.

Beep.

"Hi, this is Leonard, well, I guess you already knew that." Leonard's old girlfriend had not gotten around to changing her cell phone number yet. "Um, I was just wondering if you saw me in Sports Illustrated this week. They said I was a hero. In case you don't get the magazine at home, I took a picture of the story and texted it to you. Maybe you saw me on TV, I tried to text that to you, but I couldn't get it to work. I even have a Wikipedia page now, here, I'll read it to you. It says, Leonard Fleischmann, I need to get that changed to Leonard 'Bud' Fleischmann, but I'll do that when I..."

Beep.

"This user's voice mailbox is full."

Click.

7

SOME PEOPLE LOOKED at The Meadowlands and saw a swamp. Others saw a swamp that needed to have a huge football stadium planted in the middle of it.

The founders envisioned a venue that would stage events to stir the hearts of mankind. Twisted Sister reunion concerts, monster truck rallies, college football bowl games, the Super Bowl.

They would even let the New York Jets play there.

Despite the visions of the men who stood in that swamp and saw the future, The Meadowlands stadium spent most days very quietly save the occasional Jimmy Hoffa conspiracy theorist poking around the end zones looking for telltale signs that the legendary union boss was buried below. (He isn't. Don't ask.)

When the Meadowlands is empty, the Meadowlands isn't making money. If you came to the management with an event that would put butts in seats and lines at the concessions, they were interested. Of course, they did have standards. They rejected the International Midget-Throwing Contest (organizers expected to set the world record for most people watching live midget throwing). The pitch they were getting now wasn't much better.

"Look, this is gonna be friggin' huge," said the plaid jacket wearing promoter that went by one name.

"Call me Ralph. Just one name. Like Cher. Or Obama."

Obama?, thought Sharon, The Meadowlands marketing representative, but hey, Ralph was rolling and she didn't want to mess up his flow. After all, his credit checked out and that was good enough for her.

"This is gonna be fantastic, people are gonna be lining up all around this place. How many people can this joint hold? We're gonna pack 'em in, baby."

"82,556," Sharon said.

"Okay, maybe just the bottom deck, but we'll fill it full of people, the best kind of people, you know what I'm talking about?," Ralph said jabbing the woman in the ribs.

"No," she said, catching her breath, "I don't know what you mean."

"The best kind of people," Ralph said, leaning in, "are beer drinkers."

He had her attention now.

"Bowlers, baby, bowlers. Nobody drinks more beer than bowlers, you can look it up. And we're going to fill this joint with beer swilling bowlers."

"Did you say 'beer swilling bowlers.'"

"Yes I did."

"Please continue."

Ralph's pitch was simple. A high stakes bowling championship right in the middle of The Meadowlands. Winner take all with a million dollar prize.

"Do you have anyone lined up for the million dollar prize?," Sharon asked.

"How much can you guys kick in?", Ralph asked.

"Zero."

"Okay, maybe we'll just go with a really nice trophy. You guys have bowling lanes you can set up on the 50-yard line, right?"

"What? Bowling lanes?"

"We'll work that out later."

And Ralph did. He figured out how to get portable bowling lanes to New Jersey, scraped together a hundred grand in prize money and, best of all, the winner would get a one-year spot on the pro bowling tour.

You win, you go pro. Welcome to the big time.

And thus, the Jani-San Custodial Services 100 Grand Bowling Invitational, presented by Scratch-Eze Antifungal Spray, was born.

Ray saw the flier while he was in the men's room. Coughing up blood.

Pretty normal routine by now. Bowl a couple of frames, drink a beer, puke up some stomach lining, go back and do it again. You kind of get into a groove.

"Jesus Christ," a guy in the men's room said, "are you skinning a fucking moose in here? It looks like a crime scene."

"Aren't you Mr. Compassion. How about a little, 'Hey Ray are you okay? It doesn't seem normal to be vomiting up so much blood.'"

"Okay, hey Ray are you okay from vomiting up blood?"

"Mind your own fucking business before I shove a bowling pin up your ass."

Ray tore the flier off the wall and crammed it in his pocket. No need to make it easy for the riffraff to get involved.

One of the regional qualifiers would be right here at Massapequa Pin and Pub. He'd crush all the local guys. Ray knew the oil patterns on these lanes like he knew the buttons on his remote control. He could work both with his eyes closed.

"I don't need to see the lane," Ray would say. "I go by feel."

"You're full of crap, Ray."

Then Ray would kick their ass by twenty pins and send them on their merry way.

"What an asshole," both would mutter under their breath.

There was a very real possibility that Ray could drop dead before the event. He needed to hang on until the big tournament in order to fulfill his lifelong dream of keeling over on live television.

He could see it now. Ray is rolling a strong game, but he's a few pins behind. He gets to the tenth and, oh no, he leaves a split that he has to pick up to win by just one pin. Ray milks the scene for all it's worth, he coughs up a little blood, clearly he's hurting, but he's not giving up.

"Flanagan looks like he's in pretty rough shape," the announcer would say. Ray always pictured Verne Lundquist behind the mic. He was no Chris Schenkel, but you take what you can get.

"Verne, if I'm not mistaken, it looks like Flanagan just coughed up a piece of his liver," the color commentator would say.

"I'm no doctor, but it looks like liver to me. Flanagan seems to be at death's door. It must be taking a superhuman effort to get this far. What was his wife thinking when she left a man like that?"

"Just what I was wondering, Verne."

Ray would roll the ball slowly, surely. The scene would run in slow motion as the first pin began to fly and bounce across the lane, just glancing off the second pin. It would teeter back and forth, would it go?

"He's done it," Verne would say. "One of the greatest come from behind victories in the history of bowling. Ladies and gentlemen, we are watching history here at The Meadowlands."

Ray would hold his hands high above his head in celebration and then drop over dead. Bam. A dream come true.

There was only one thing that could come between Ray and his dream of dropping dead on television. That know-it-all kid from the pro shop, Leonard.

He'd seen the kid bowl and the kid had something. If Ray bowled by feel, this guy was a technician. He looked at the lane like a doctor looking at a rash. His form was perfect. Every time he threw the ball he looked just like the little gold guy on the top of a bowling trophy. A shorter, slightly fatter version, but pretty much the same.

But the kid didn't have the guts, wasn't tough enough for the big time. Ray wouldn't have to outbowl him, but he would have to intimidate him. And if that didn't work, he'd just break his hands.

Ray's mind wandered to pastoral scenes of the northern New Jersey swamplands. Specifically, he wondered if he'd be able to drink beer while bowling in the Jani-San Custodial Services 100 Grand Bowling

Invitational, presented by Scratch-Eze Antifungal Spray. Probably. Hell, it's New Jersey, you can drink beer while you're having a colonoscopy.

Who the heck would want to bowl in The Meadowlands, Leonard thought, his bowling brain shifting into overdrive. It's outdoors, the elements would play havoc with lane conditions. The patterns would change every frame. How would they return the balls? Would they have ball boys like in tennis? How much would the parking be?

Leonard had questions, lots of questions. But he knew one thing, this was his chance and he was ready to take it. Sure, he was the club pro, but he would have to win the qualifier just like anyone else.

He started to size up the competition. There were a couple of league guys who might get lucky and win, but it's pretty hard to keep the luck going in an elimination tournament. Usually the beer and the hot dogs caught up with those guys. They didn't have the discipline to fall back on.

Except that one guy, Flanagan. What an asshole. The last time Leonard tried to chat up Ray and give him a pointer or two, it didn't go so well.

"Nice game you're rolling there, Mr. Flanagan," Leonard said.

"Yeah."

"If you don't mind me saying, if you adjusted your footwork a little, you might be able to make some real improvements."

"I don't remember asking you."

"Just trying to be the helpful club pro."

"Why don't you get lost before I help you to a broken jaw, you fat, Jewish prick."

They weren't exactly forging a friendship for the ages.

Leonard had to admit, the guy could bowl. Ray was a power bowler. He had a strong back and arms from years of loading and unloading trucks. The man had God-given athletic skills he had spent the better part of five decades drowning in booze. Despite that, he still carried an average most pro bowlers would be proud to have. Even worse, the man seemed completely impervious to pressure. He bowled like today was his last day on earth. Leonard envied that, but he vowed to beat him. He had to.

8

"A HUNDRED THOUSAND DOLLARS?," roared Dale Saxby, the CEO of Jani-San, the country's third-largest supplier of janitorial supplies and services. Their name was at the bottom of half the urinals coast to coast.

"Do you know how much money that is?"

"Duh, it's a hundred thousand dollars," said Dale, Jr., his son and Chief Marketing Officer.

Making his son Chief Marketing Officer was his wife's idea. Ever since he glued elbow macaroni to an empty soup can and painted it gold back in the second grade she thought he was a creative genius.

The fact was, Dale, Jr. was an idiot. Even worse, he was a lazy idiot. It's a harsh thing to say about your boy, but Dale Saxby was nothing if not honest. His 23-year-old son had graduated college with a B.A. in Marketing and an emphasis on screwing up. He totaled a Jaguar, a BMW, a Lexus and a fully restored 1972 Ford Bronco (his mother thought a truck would be safer). So far, the used Nissan Altima hadn't been wrapped around a tree or needed to be pulled out of the living room of a frat house, but he'd only been driving it for two months.

Dale's original idea was to put his son in the

marketing department so he couldn't cause any trouble like he did when he worked in the warehouse during college.

One night Dale, Jr. and his frat brothers decided to pull a prank by using some acid to etch a different frat's Greek letters into the football field, cleverly getting the other guys in trouble. The kind of brilliant plan only a sale on Natural Light beer could produce. Dale, Jr. figured 20 gallon bottles of muriatic acid should do the trick. Not that he knew anything about chemicals, he just unlocked the Jani-San warehouse and grabbed anything with the word acid in the name.

The football field prank went great, so they decided to get some more beer and burn the words "Suck It" into the lawn of the president's house. That's when they saw Dale, Jr.'s BMW surrounded by the campus police in full SWAT gear.

Turns out Dale, Jr., who had polished off a 12-pack that night already, had been playing a little fast and loose with the acid bottles. He threw one of them into the trunk of the BMW without realizing the cap was a little loose. The acid slowly leaked out, ate through the floor pan, into the electrical system and caused a short circuit that set off the BMW's alarm.

Real police departments don't respond to car alarms. Campus cops do.

When Dale and the Pi Kappa Alpha boys came running out of the tunnel of the football stadium wearing black ski masks and ironic t-shirts, they were greeted by the screeching BMW and the campus SWAT team jumping out of the bed of a Ford pick up usually used by the landscaping crew. Next budget year they were getting an armored personnel carrier.

"Is this your car?," the policeman asked one of the

brothers.

"Nope, it's his," he said, selling Dale, Jr. down the river without a moment's hesitation.

"Hey, wait a minute," the policeman said, his voice muffled by the face shield of his riot helmet, "what were you guys doing in the stadium? And why are you carrying those bottles?"

Two hours later the master sleuths had cracked the case and Dale senior was throwing bail for his son and four of his idiot friends. Or as he called them now, the Jani-San marketing department.

"What made you think putting up one hundred thousand dollars in cash for a bowling tournament was a good idea," Dale said. "How could this possibly benefit us?"

"Dad, it's in New Jersey," Dale, Jr. countered.

"And?"

"New Jersey is filthy."

Dale had to admit the boy had a point.

"I'll give you that, but do people who buy janitorial supplies watch bowling tournaments?"

"How the hell should I know? Is it cool if the marketing department has a team building meeting in Atlantic City before the tournament? Hope so, because we already put down a non-refundable deposit."

There was no way Dale was losing a hundred thousand dollars on a New Jersey bowling tournament. No way in hell. He couldn't cancel the contract, it was ironclad. The event already had a website and everything. He couldn't ask his suppliers to kick in, they'd know what his insane son was up to. There was only one way to hang on to that money, he was going to have to win it.

That would require cheating. And that would require the Duval brothers.

Dale hated calling the Duval brothers. A loose cannon on a wet deck. Times two.

But they had their place. They were like the Mr. Fix-It handymen of the petty crime world. They'd do whatever you needed done and, this was Dale's favorite part, they did it at discounted prices.

The man had a business to run after all.

And when there was a problem that was outside the normal channels (meaning "illegal"), he called in the Duval brothers. A hundred thousand dollars was definitely outside the normal channels. It might cost him five or ten grand, but he'd save ninety. You didn't have to be Donald Trump to see that was a good deal.

He picked up his cell and punched in a number for Jackson, Mississippi. It picked up on the third ring.

"Hello," the voice said.

Thank God, Dale thought, I got the smart one. This will go a lot faster.

"Hey Jimmy, it's Dale over in Texas, how are you?"

"Dale, you don't give two shits about how I am, you only call when you want something."

"But I always pay, don't I?"

"That's why I picked up the phone."

"How's your brother?"

"Really Dale? You don't even give a single shit how my brother is."

"Just making conversation."

"Don't bother."

"Got a job for you boys."

"We're super busy."

Dale rolled his eyes. Jimmy and Timmy were always busy. Usually they were trying to figure out how to rob the post office or like last year when they were busy plotting the kidnapping of Mark Burnet, the guy who created the reality TV show "Survivor."

"Are you kidding me," Jimmy said. "They'll pay a shitload of money to get that guy back. He invented the Tribal Council. The Tribal fucking Council."

"I bet they'll pay twenty grand," Timmy said. They were not shoot for the stars kind of guys.

"Sorry to hear that, Jimmy," Dale said, "what are you boys up to?"

"I shouldn't be telling you this, Dale, 'cause it's big. Really big. Hugest score ever."

"Yeah, you probably shouldn't tell me."

"Okay, since you twisted my arm, I'll tell you. We're gonna go to Atlanta, break into the big vault at the Coca-Cola Museum and steal the dadgum recipe for Coke."

Dale needed a minute to let that one soak in.

"No chance they may have it written down somewhere else?"

"How did you get to be so successful when you're so dumb? They'll want to keep it out of the wrong hands. I figure if Coke won't pay us to get it back, the guys at RC Cola will cough up fifty or sixty grand for it."

"Not to mention the guys at Pepsi."

"Pepsi? Holy shit!," he put his hand over the mouthpiece and shouted at his brother. "Timmy, we could sell the recipe to Pepsi. You know what Dale, you're not a dumb shit ALL of the time."

"Just trying to help you guys out any way I can. Think you might have time to squeeze in a little work for me on the way to Atlanta?"

Two 36-year-old men, sitting on a worn out sofa in a single wide trailer in Jackson, Mississippi. One about five foot ten, one about six foot six. One named Jimmy, one named Timmy. One white, one black. Two brothers who did everything together. They were ready to go to work. As soon as Maury was over. It was one of those Who's Your Baby Daddy episodes. They weren't about to miss that. And it gave them plenty of time to load up the guns, grab some beef jerky and get ready to roll.

9

YOU'VE NEVER SEEN the Wisco Bowling Security Team, but, rest assured, they've seen you.

With a system so technologically advanced it's the stuff of the NSA director's wet dreams, the Wisco Bowling Security Team knows every game you've ever rolled, every pin you've ever hit, what kind of ball you throw, what size shoe you wear and how much you've spent on bowling. To the penny.

Bowlers celebrated years ago when alleys switched over from pencil and paper scoring with people counting pins on their fingers and toes to the automated computer scoring systems so common today. What those bowlers didn't know was that every one of those machines sent a data feed to a small office in a sub-sub basement of the Wisco world headquarters in Waukesha, Wisconsin.

If you're rolling a good game it sets off an alert in the basement. Thanks to predictive computer technology, the Wisco people know about your 300 game before you do. And when someone is closing in on a perfect 900 series, the office shuts down and watches through hidden cameras in the scoring screens.

They also have another tool. They can affect the

outcome of games if they want.

An avid bowler named Bill Fong, a regular at the Plano Super Bowl in Plano, Texas, a suburb of Dallas, was on track for a 900 series. Three perfect games in a row, the ultimate goal for any league bowler.

It all came down to the tenth frame of the third game, one strike away from glory. Fewer than 30 people have bowled a 900 series. Ever. It usually means an automatic contract from one of the big bowling companies, a shot at going on the tour and a place in the bowling record books. The entire bowling alley, all 48 lanes, stopped to watch what surely would be Plano Super Bowl history.

Fong rolled the ball right on line, it spun correctly, grabbed the lane at the perfect point and turned straight into the pocket. He could feel it, he could smell the strike. The pins flew around, but when the smoke cleared, one pin was still standing.

What he didn't know, couldn't know and never would know, is that someone in the sub-sub basement in Waukesha had pressed the red button. Not unlike the system deployed in nuclear missile silos, the red button required two operators to turn separate key locks and enter a code number that is kept in a safe under 24-hour guard.

Once the red button is pressed, something happens in the pinsetting machine in the chosen bowling center on the selected lane. What looks like a normal hydraulic actuator is really a hidden compartment containing a pin much heavier than a regulation pin. It's scuffed and marked and scarred to blend in with the other pins, but it won't move like the other pins. It makes a strike virtually impossible.

After the frame is thrown, the pinsetting machine

shuts down and shows an error code that can only be reset by a Wisco factory rep. A tactical team is sent out to retrieve the pin and keep the secret safe.

On that night at the Plano Super Bowl the system worked like a charm. Sure, a bowler had his lifelong dreams crushed, but he was just an unfortunate victim in the war to preserve the game they all loved.

The Wisco Bowling Security Team regarded themselves as the Knights Templar of bowling. Super secret, independent and, if necessary, above the law. They were put on the planet to protect and preserve the game of ten-pin bowling and would go to any extreme in order to do so.

Up to and including murder. The last time was in 1979.

Dr. John Adler, a general practitioner and avid bowler, turned his back on the sport. After hurting his elbow in a tournament one night (he was a lowly 145 average bowler according to Wisco security records), he started looking at bowling related injuries. He believed the repetitive motion with a heavy weight at the end of the arm was causing a spate of elbow and wrist injuries. Adler calculated the injuries were costing American businesses two billion dollars a year in lost productivity. He published a newsletter, went on some news shows and was scheduled to testify before the International Olympic Committee as they debated allowing bowling into the Olympic Games.

That testimony would never happen.

The night before he was scheduled to testify, two men in black suits and dark sunglasses came to his door.

"Can I help you?," said the doctor.

"We'd like you to come with us," said the one man

in the black suit.

"And who the hell are you?"

"We're representatives from the American Bowling Congress."

"You're lying."

"Yes we are."

With that, the second black suited thug threw a bag over the doctor's head and they jammed him into the trunk of a nondescript Oldsmobile sedan rented with cash and fake IDs.

Dr. Adler's body was never found, but the gray sand in the ashtrays at his local bowling alley did have a strangely familiar sense about it.

Members of the Wisco Security Team were deep under cover. They did not reveal their real jobs to friends or family, they did not talk about their work with anyone. Each member was issued a cover story about being in the Marketing Department or Accounting. The members didn't even know each other's real names.

They identified each other by their bowling averages.

Ms. 191 was assigned to the Bernie Steers case. She was a born bowler with a pro level average and a power swing that belied her slight five foot two inch frame. One of the very few members of the team who could go undercover as a pro at a moment's notice.

Her partner was Mr. 176. A total meathead with no form and lots of strength, but when things got tough he was handy to have around. Trained in three forms of military-style hand-to-hand combat, just about every handheld weapons system in existence and big as a house. Their Wisco-issued armor-plated black Suburban had two rocket propelled grenades in the back. If they ever needed them, Mr. 176 could make them sing. Maybe he should start bowling with RPGs, she thought, it would probably help his average.

Bernie Steers had been on 191's radar screen for a long, long time. The other engineers thought he was an anti-social crackpot, 191 knew better. She had unfettered access to his computer screen, all his files and all his experiments. 191 knew Bernie was getting close. Very close.

He was working on something that would revolutionize bowling, something the Wisco marketing guys would salivate over, that bowling alleys would dream of having and that those bastards over at Pinknockerz would kill for.

The world's first self-correcting bowling ball.

It looked and rolled like a regular bowling ball, but that's where the similarities ended. Steers had gone off the deep end and crossed the line to the dark side of bowling ball engineering.

Deep inside the ball was a series of accelerometers that sensed how fast you threw the ball, the rate and direction of spin and where the ball was on the lane in relation to the pins. Instead of a solid core, the ball had an oblong cavity filled with a viscous fluid and a series of carbon fiber micropumps that could reconfigure the ball a thousand times per second.

The cover could also change by generating an electrical force that would make the cover ever so slightly more grippy or less grippy depending on how the sensors read the lane. The systems were only activated while the ball was in motion, so it could pass any standard test short of actually cutting the ball open.

That meant the ball could read any lane, know where it was at any time and instantly create the perfect hook to drive into the pocket. Every single time.

A blind man could roll a 180 with it.

Bernie never bowled more than a few frames with the ball, because he was afraid to attract too much attention. He knew what he had and, in many ways, viewed himself as the Dr. Robert Oppenheimer of the bowling world. Steers had invented the equivalent of a nuclear bomb and he didn't know what it might do to the game he loved.

Then there was her boss, Mr. 221. He had given over his life to bowling. No family, no relationships, no friends, no hobbies. His rise to the head of the Wisco Security Team was inevitable, almost destined. And he did the job as naturally as he breathed in and out. 221 had also been following Bernie's work. Very closely. Certainly more closely than Wisco had followed him.

Had the Wisco Security Team looked a little harder at one of their own trusted members, they would have noticed the monthly five thousand dollar deposits going into his checking account from the Paraplegic Bowlers of America (the "other PBA" as they liked to refer to themselves). An organization that, on its surface, sponsored bowling activities for wounded veterans who had lost the use of their legs, but, in reality, served as a front group for Pinknockerz's secret activities.

Mr. 221 was a mole. And he was about to deliver beyond his employer's wildest imagination.

When Bernie disappeared, security at both companies went on full alert, but Bernie was in the wind, no one could find him. Because they weren't looking in the most obvious place.

A strange thing happened at the regional qualifier for the Jani-San 100 Grand Invitational, sponsored by Scratch-Eze Antifungal Spray being held at the Wantagh Fun Center in Long Island. A small man with a mustache and what appeared to be a woman's blond wig done in the style of Farrah Fawcett dominated the tournament with a 280-300-260 series.

He name was listed as Sternie Beers.

10

"KILL LEONARD," said Uncle Sally.

"You really want me to send Leonard to sleep with the fishes?," said the Crock Pot with equal measures of glee and horror.

"Sleep with the fishes? Are you in some kind of idiot time warp? It isn't 1937."

"Sorry, Uncle Sally."

"Every time that kid picks up a bowling ball, there's a reporter in here asking him how he saved the fucking day. And when you have three dead Russian mob guys and a Zamboni-sized hole in your wall, you also got every cop in the tri-state area crawling up your ass."

"He's a really good bowler, Uncle Sally. And a hero for saving your life. Look what he's done for bowling."

"That's the problem, stunod. This place is packed day and night. They want us to open up 24/7 so we can cram more people in. We're making a fortune. It's killing my business."

Uncle Sally had big problems. With Leonard's newfound fame, Massapequa Pin and Pub was jammed. There were leagues every day and night, they were selling tons of food and booze. Raising the prices didn't help, people were still flocking to the place.

Even the pro shop, guaranteed to fail as long as Leonard was running it, was making money hand over fist.

The bowling alley that had been producing nice, clean losses to help him launder cash from numbers, prostitution and other business interests had turned into a cash-making machine. Making cash meant paying taxes and paying taxes meant lots of questions.

Uncle Sally didn't like questions.

"Kill him, Crock Pot. I'm counting on you," said Uncle Sally.

"Screw the Crock Pot, Uncle Sally, I'll take care of it," offered Big Mike.

"Who are you kidding? You got your shooting arm in a sling, your foot is wrapped up in some kind of medical erector set and you're wearing an eye patch. Jesus, Mary and Joseph, you'd be lucky to kill time."

Uncle Sally had a point. One orthopedic surgeon put a couple of stainless steel screws into Big Mike's shoulder to hold the tendons back together while another one put an external fixator on his foot to hold the pieces of his pinkie toe in place. Mikey was left stomping around in a plastic boot with a series of metal rods, screws and cables sticking out of the side.

Then there was the eye patch.

The doctors didn't think the vision was ever coming back. He shared that bad news with some of the guys and they started calling him Deadeye Mike. Fucking perfect.

"C'mon, boss, I can get it done."

"The only thing you're getting done around here is raising our health insurance. Try not to spend any more time in hospitals and let the Crock Pot do this."

"Do I have to bring Uncle Frank this time?," the Crock Pot asked.

"Get it done tomorrow. And if you ask me one more question I'll kill you and Leonard."

Which, oddly enough, was exactly what Big Mike was planning to do.

I'm going to have to kill Leonard, thought Ray Flanagan.

He had never killed anyone before.

Not on purpose, anyway.

Now Ray wished that when he was in the Army he would have paid more attention when they talked about how to kill people.

Still, how hard could it be to kill Leonard? He was the least dangerous man Ray had ever met. Just follow him home from the bowling alley and shoot him or hit him with a board or something. His girlfriend dumped him, Al would be happy if the guy didn't show up at work, nobody would report him missing for days.

Of course, Ray could make this a win-win for everybody. Ray was an idea guy and he was in the middle of a brainstorm. He would just make Leonard brain dead by hitting him in the head really hard. He joked about that with the VA lady on the phone, but now he was kind of liking the idea. Ray would hit Leonard in the alley behind the Pin and Pub and call an ambulance right away. That way they could keep Leonard's organs alive. The next day Ray would just casually call and ask if any livers had become available locally.

Leonard was kind of fat and short, after a few rough calculations, Ray figured Leonard's liver would be a reasonably good fit. Assuming he hit him in the head and not in the liver. He could use the pointy side of a claw hammer, but no, Ray really needed the claw hammer. Bowling ball? Kind of cliché. Wait a minute, how about a hockey stick with Russian writing on it? Then the cops would think it was a revenge killing from the Russian mob. Ray didn't even know what the Russian mob did (smuggle Vodka?), so the cops would never suspect.

He'd take Leonard out tomorrow.

"Here's the plan," Dale from Jani-San started. "You find somebody who can win that goddamn bowling tournament and then just flat out get rid of everybody else who even has a chance."

"You mean kill 'em?," Jimmy Duval said on the phone.

"Goddammit Jimmy," Dale screamed. "Have you ever heard of the NSA?"

"The space guys? Are they bowling in space?"

"No, the spying guys."

"Like the CIA?"

"Yes, like the CIA."

"Then why don't they just call it the CIA?"

"I don't know, Jimmy, but they listen in on all our phone calls. Everybody in America. And when they hear people saying things like 'kill' and 'bomb' and 'drug deal' they tend to get really upset."

"So I shouldn't say you want to give me money to

kill off some bowler dude?"

Dale just sighed. This is what happens when you hire a couple of heavies off Craig's List.

He figured you could find anything on Craig's List, so just for a lark, he looked under "jobs/general labor" and found the ad from the Duval Brothers.

"Jimmy and Timmy Duval are available for all sorts of odd jobs. Odder the better. Which side of the law it's on doesn't matter much to us as long as it pays in cash. Interests in kidnapping, blackmail, breaking and entering and con jobs. No foreigners. No pets. Reasonable prices."

If the cops ever bothered to look at Craig's List they could fill up the jails without ever leaving their desks.

It was the last two words of their ad that caught Dale's attention. He was nothing if not cheap and he liked to work with people who shared his enthusiasm for thrift. Even if it meant almost constant disappointment which Jimmy and Timmy almost always delivered.

When local janitors in Texarkana, Arkansas threatened to unionize, he sent the boys up there to knock some heads. Despite their efforts, the union won an overwhelming victory.

"We were supposed to tell them to vote no?," Jimmy said. "Shit, sorry Dale, we got that backwards."

Even so, the boys were hardworking and, if guided properly, would get the job done. Maybe. But you could always count on the final bill being very reasonable. They had standards.

"I've done some Googling on this tournament and found a couple of guys that might be good targets to either flip to our side or get rid of."

"You mean kill?"

"For crying out loud, Jimmy."

"Sorry. If anyone's listening, I didn't mean that."

"There are two guys up in New York. One's called Sternie Beers and he just kicked ass in a tournament in a place called Wantagh, however you say it. I don't know why they can't just have American names up there. And there's another guy named Leonard Fleischman."

"The guy who killed the Russian mob thugs with a bowling ball? I saw that on TMZ."

"Yeah him."

"We'll try to get them to work for us and if we don't we should..."

"Don't say kill him again. Oh crap."

"C'mon Dale, you're gonna piss off NASA."

The Wisco Security Team had very simple orders. Find Bernie Steers and the self-correcting bowling ball. Make sure the ball doesn't fall in to evil hands. Especially Pinknockerz hands. Shoot, if necessary. Shoot to kill.

11

MASSAPEQUA PIN AND PUB did not make the list of Top Ten Places to Find Your Mate in Nassau County. They wouldn't have made the list if it went to a thousand. A bowling alley is not a place to find eligible mates. Unless you're under 12 or over 60, there's not much of a dating pool at a bowling alley.

When Leonard spotted a woman about his age walk in, it got his attention right away. She had all her arms and legs, didn't appear to be homeless, he wondered if she was meeting someone or maybe got off at the wrong bus stop. She was carrying a old public television canvas tote bag that had stenciled on the side, "A Rare Medium Well Done." It clearly had a bowling ball in it.

Wearing a hat and dark sunglasses, she walked up to the counter like she owned the place. Al took her money while trying to look down her shirt and then turned around to check out her ass as she walked over to the lane. Solid class.

The woman pulled out a pair of beat and battered bowling shoes and then a beautiful blue Pinknockerz Pincracker ball. Aggressive choice, Leonard thought.

Then she started to bowl. Leonard found himself staring at her through the pro shop window. He could tell she wasn't bowling for a score, she was working on something like a real bowler would. Her footwork or maybe her release, Leonard couldn't tell. She was a good bowler for sure, but with a little help and the right coach, she could be great.

Leonard's history with women was spotty at best. Okay, it was terrible. He dated a girl in high school who changed her college choice three times to make sure she didn't go to the same school as Leonard did.

"We can make a long distance relationship work," she told Leonard. Then failed to give him her address. He thought it was odd for a Speech Therapy major to attend the Colorado School of Mines, but he figured she knew what she was doing.

Then there was his last relationship. He thought she was the one, but it turns out she didn't have the intestinal fortitude to live the life of a professional athlete's partner.

"You and that stupid bowling make me want to throw up," she said. "When are you going to grow up and get a real job?"

She did not regard being the club pro at Massapequa Pin and Pub as a real job.

"Leonard, if you sing Happy Birthday to seven-year-olds you do not have a career."

"Hosting birthday parties is an important part of my job. Those seven-year-olds, if you treat them well, will come back to be good, regular bowling customers."

"Oh great, so you can look forward to shooting antifungal spray into their smelly shoes in a few years."

"Again with the shoes."

Leonard was now a man on his own. A famous

man on his own. He enjoyed the notoriety, but it was a distraction from working on his game. With the regional qualifier coming up he had work to do and couldn't be distracted by women. Still, fate had put the perfect woman 20 feet away from him.

He knew he wasn't very good with women, so he hesitated. Then he thought, hey, I'm the club pro here, I can talk to the bowlers and offer some help here and there. He did something he never did before. Leonard went for it.

"You gonna go set up for the bar mitzvah?," Al shouted at Leonard as he exited the pro shop.

"Not now, Al."

Al wanted to make sure Leonard got the damn bar mitzvah stuff set up before the Crock Pot killed him. Al hated dealing with parties. The bad news was that Al was going to have to find someone else to do all the crap work around the bowling alley. On the good news side, tomorrow was the fifteenth and, assuming the Crock Pot didn't screw this up, Al wouldn't have to write Leonard another paycheck.

Leonard closed in on the woman on Lane 18. He just stood there for a second watching her roll. He started to say something, but, as usual, he had no opening line. Finally, she scooped her Pincracker out of the ball return and looked straight at Leonard.

"Hi," he said.

"Hello," she answered.

"Nice ball."

"Really? You pick up a lot of girls with that line?"

"No, I, uh, I just like your ball."

"I have to say, no one's ever come on to me with that one before, so you're unique."

"No, really, the Pincracker 2. Good, aggressive

choice. I like it."

"So you're not hitting on me?"

Leonard had no answer.

"Sorry," she said, "it's just that if you're a single woman under the age of one hundred and you're in a bowling alley, you get used to every creepy old guy hitting on you. At least you're not old. Jury's still out on the creepy part."

"I'm Leonard Fleischman, the club pro here, but you can call me Bud."

"I like Leonard better."

"Leonard it is."

To be honest, Leonard would have gone with Betty Jo if that's what she wanted.

"Your footwork is excellent," he said.

"You're not one of those weirdo foot fetish guys are you?"

"What? No. Your footwork, five-step approach, strong, but smooth."

"Okay, so you know what you're talking about."

"I've never seen you in here before."

"Another great bowling alley pick up line?"

"That one never works, either."

Leonard was really starting to like her.

"My name is Susie," she said, sticking out her right hand with the wrist support still on it. She had a firm handshake developed from years of throwing a 12-pounder.

"Would you like to go out sometime?," Leonard couldn't believe he heard himself say that.

"You have a Wisco logo on your shirt, are you sure you're allowed to go out with a Pinknockerz bowler?"

"I think a mixed marriage could work."

"When?"

"How about tonight? I'm done here at the bowling alley at 7. I can come pick you up."

"Slow down, cowboy, I'll just meet you here."

Leonard had a real live date. With a girl. Who bowled. The rest of the day he happily unclogged toilets and lit birthday candles and didn't react to any of the crass comments Al tossed his way. Leonard had to get ready.

Where do you take the girl of your dreams on a first date?

"You gotta go Italian," Al said. "It's the food of romance."

"I thought French was the food of romance," Leonard said.

"No, French is the food of people who don't take showers. It's disgusting."

"You need to take her to Nonna Cocina."

"Seriously Al? I want her to like me."

"You don't know shit about food."

But Leonard knew plenty about Nonna Cocina, an Italian restaurant that claimed to be "Just like eating at Grandma's house." They delivered on that promise.

The entire restaurant was owned, run and staffed by little Italian grandmas as a way to get jobs for their lazy sons and rich husbands for their ugly daughters. They also served food. Anyone who has spent any time with little Italian grandmas knows that one Italian grandma is a wonderful blessing, but two Italian grandmas is a small scale war.

"She put sugar in the tomato sauce?," Wednesday's grandma would say about Tuesday's grandma's cooking techniques. "Madonna mi! Did she learn to cook yesterday? What will she cook tomorrow? Corn flakes Parmesan? Here, try this, it's what sauce is supposed to taste like."

The little Italian grandmas would stay in the kitchen and fight, while the lazy sons ran the front of the house, flirted with the patrons and drank free wine from the bar.

On Leonard's last visit, the waiter was taking Leonard's order with a cigarette in his mouth and a cell phone trapped between his cheek and shoulder.

"What do you want? No, no, hang on, I'm talking to a customer. I don't care what you want. Ha, ha! Hang on, baby."

"How is the lasagna tonight?"

"It's good every night."

"Have you tried it."

"I don't have to try it, I know it's good just by looking at it."

"Have you looked at it?"

"No."

"I'll try it."

Two minutes later the waiter was heading back to Leonard's table, only this time he was walking bent over sideways at a 45 degree angle. This was because he was being led out of the kitchen by a four-foot tall Italian grandma clutching his ear and holding a wooden spoon.

"Did you let this man order lasagna?"

"Yeah, mama, that's what he wanted."

"What's a matter with you? Look at the belly on him. He's had enough lasagna, no?"

"I didn't really look at him, I was on the phone with Isabella."

She smacked him on the back of the head so hard it knocked off his Prada sunglasses. "Why are you talking to Isabella? She's divorced with two kids, she's no good for you, stunod!"

Then to Leonard she said, "How about a nice salad and a Bronzino? We'll trim you down a little."

Leonard never even got a chance to see the dessert menu. Nonna Cocina was definitely off the list. He would take Susie to his no-miss place, the Cheesecake Factory. You can't go wrong with cheesecake.

The pro shop was shut down, the last of the bar mitzvah flotsam and jetsam was cleaned up, a new Wisco bowling polo shirt was picked out and by 6:55 Leonard was ready and waiting.

Susie arrived at 7:10, she wanted to make him sweat a little, but not too much. She kinda liked this guy, he seemed sweet.

"You ready?," he asked.

"To get out of this bowling alley? Yes, I'm ready."

"We'll go out the back door, my car's out there."

They stepped out the back door and never saw the guy with the shovel.

12

NO ONE EXPECTS TO GET HIT in the head with a shovel. It's not on the normal list of things to be on the lookout for. Especially when you're planning to kill someone.

The Crock Pot was determined to make his first solo hit a winner and he hadn't given up on trying to get his nickname changed to One Bullet. If Big Mike could morph into Deadeye Mike, he could shake the Crock Pot name, too. This had to go smoothly. No problems. No complications.

He really hated to kill Leonard, he was a good guy, they had talked bowling, but this wasn't personal, it was business. He loved saying that, there wasn't a more mob movie line in the world. One slug racked into his camouflage Wal-Mart shotgun and he was ready to get to work.

The plan was simple. He knew Leonard would walk out right at 7 pm. The Crock Pot would pump a round into his chest, grab his wallet and take off. The cops would think it was a senseless murder/robbery that would have the added benefit of hurting the bowling alley's business, because people would think it was too dangerous to go there. Uncle Sally would be thrilled to have a dead body bleeding out behind the building.

Crock Pot would hide behind Leonard's car and blast him right there. Then he'd hop in his own car and casually drive away like nothing happened. Cold, calculating. One Bullet. Or Slugger. Slugger could be a good nickname, since he was knocking people off with slugs. He actually liked that better because it freed him up to carry more than one shell. That's what was going through his mind as he stepped out the back door of the bowling alley. Those thoughts were interrupted by another, more urgent thought. Is that a shovel?

Ray figured this would be a piece of cake. He knew Leonard got off work at seven. He'd seen him walk out the back door and get in his piece of shit Dodge Neon plenty of times before. So all Ray had to do was wait until the door opened, smack him with the shovel in such a way that he was a brain dead vegetable with a really useful liver. How hard could it be?

At 6:59 Ray stood in the shadows by the back door of Massapequa Pin and Pub. He heard the latch on the door start to move, so he reached high overhead with his shovel and as soon as he saw Leonard come out he brought it down like a sledgehammer.

Only it wasn't Leonard. Although the guy kinda looked like him and Ray had a couple of pops already. The guy was pudgy, kinda young, but instead of a polo shirt and carrying a bowling bag, he was wearing a sport coat and carrying a camouflage pump shotgun. Ray had started the swing already and there was no way he could stop. He did what he could to take a little power off and managed to land a glancing blow to the guy's head.

Blood gushed everywhere as the guy staggered backward. Natural reflex caused his hand clenched around the shotgun to flex and fire off the slug. It neatly peeled off Ray's left ear on its way to shooting out two letters of the neon sign above that was now advertising the fact that Massapequa Pin and Pub was equipped with a Bar & ill.

"Shit, you shot me, you fat fuck."

The Crock Pot, rapidly losing both consciousness and blood, could only manage, "Ugh."

Ray dropped the shovel, picked up the shotgun and stumbled back to his truck leaving a long, red trail of blood.

Seconds later the door opened again putting Leonard and Susie in the middle of the bloody scene. They called 911. The Cheesecake Factory would have to wait.

"Nice first date," Susie said.

For the Crock Pot it was a good news, bad news kind of story. The good news was that he wasn't far from a Level 1 trauma center, so he was stabilized right away. The bad news was that he had government healthcare. He remembered signing up for the Bronze level so he could save a few bucks. After an extensive walletectomy, the doctors decided to take a somewhat casual approach to Crock Pot's treatment.

The shovel had basically opened up his head with

a gash going from the top of his scalp, over his right eye and down his cheek. It had torn through the muscles leaving him with the ability to control only one side of his face. And instead of summoning a plastic surgeon to neatly rebuild his face, they just had an intern knock it back together with 50 or 60 staples. He looked like he'd been attacked by a gang of mailroom boys armed with red Swinglines.

And for now, at least, he had an eye patch.

He was also going to have a nasty scar and would never be able to smile normally for the rest of his life, but on the plus side he looked like a certified badass. Still, the Crock Pot's mother was pissed. She let Uncle Sally have it.

"How could you let this happen to my boy, Sally? How could you?"

"What am I supposed to do, walk him to the bus stop? Somebody mugged him right behind the bowling alley."

"You were supposed to take care of him."

"Okay, look, I gotta go. I'm supposed to get a plaque from some orphans or something."

Big Mike was loving every minute of this. He used his good arm to jam the Crock Pot up against the wall.

"Now we're even you son of a bitch," Mike hissed. "We'll see who gets the job done first."

"Listen Mike," said the Crock Pot using only half his mouth and sounding like he was shot full of Novocain, "the job's not up for grabs, Uncle Sally said it was mine."

"Say a word to Uncle Sally and I'll take the other eye. With a butter knife."

Mike was a people person.

The Cheesecake Factory does not keep formal records regarding the number of relationships that have been launched in their restaurants. With the manager's approval they will stash a diamond engagement ring in a piece of New York cheesecake. This is, of course, against the health code, but even health inspectors believe in love.

Tonight there would be no engagement ring, just an awkward first date that began with finding a semi-conscious man in a growing pool of blood.

"You really know how to treat a girl," Susie said.

"I aim to please."

"To be honest, this is right in line with how my life has been going lately."

"What do you mean?"

"My dad went missing and my mom is freaking out."

"Is it normal for your dad to go missing? I had an uncle that used to go on benders all the time."

"My dad has never touched a drink. He's an engineer. Sometimes, when he's working on something important, he'll stay at the office for a few days, but they haven't seen him at work. So I've been out looking for him."

"Where's he work?"

"In Wisconsin."

"I'm no detective, but this isn't Wisconsin."

"Very observant, grasshopper, A charge from a bowling alley in the area showed up on his credit card. My mom told the cops, but they're not exactly starting a nationwide manhunt to find a bowling ball engineer."

"Bowling ball engineer?"

"Yeah, he works at Wisco designing bowling balls. Super nerd."

"Wait a minute. If your dad does all this cutting edge stuff at Wisco, why do you have a Pinknockerz? Isn't that like sleeping with the enemy?"

"I got it just to piss him off."

"That would do it."

"If I could find him, I'd switch in a minute."

Knight in shining armor visions smashed through Leonard's head. How perfect was this? A damsel in distress who loves bowling. Don't mess this up, Leonard don't mess this up.

"I'll help you, we'll find him. Together."

"I hope so. But I'm gonna miss that ball."

13

LORRAINE STEERS WONDERED if bullets had expiration dates. Maybe somewhere printed on each shell were the words "Shoot by" and then the date. These were pretty old. No way they were newer than 1982. The year Lorraine and Bernie were married.

"Listen, Pumpkin," Lorraine's father told her right before the wedding, "take this, just in case."

From the pocket of his powder blue tuxedo slacks he produced a weathered, old snubnose revolver and held it out to her.

"Daddy, why do I need a gun?"

"To protect yourself."

"From what?"

"Burglars, robbers, kidnappers, Bernie."

"Bernie?"

"Honey, look, I know you love Bernie, but these bowling guys, they're different. Wild, unpredictable. They live life ten pins at a time, you know what I mean?"

"I have no idea what you're talking about."

"Take the gun. Just in case. Put it in your pocket."

"I'm wearing a wedding dress."

"A hundred and ninety-five dollars and it doesn't even have pockets?"

"Dad."

"Hide it in your bouquet. Just make sure you don't throw it at the reception."

"Dad."

"Okay, I'll bring it over when you come back from your honeymoon."

And that's how a 50-year-old Colt Detective Special pistol with 35-year-old bullets wound up in Lorraine's underwear drawer.

The fact that Bernie had been missing for three days was why that gun was in her hand.

There had been no word from Bernie, no word from the police and no word from the creepy security people from Wisco who acted weird when she asked them for a business card. They just mumbled something about being in touch. They had not been in touch.

She remembered Susie saying something about going off to a weekend bowling tournament – typical Susie, vanishing whenever any kind of family commitment came up – so Lorraine had nothing but time to worry about what might have happened to Bernie.

Was he kidnapped? Was he killed? Was he being tortured for the bowling ball secrets he kept in his head? Did he run off with a hot Swedish bowling instructor? Did such a thing even exist?

Lorraine had spent her entire life sitting by phones waiting for them to ring. Boyfriends. Children. Washing machine repairmen. Everyone except the cable guy, he wouldn't call no matter how long you waited. The waiting stopped now. If the police wouldn't do anything, she would.

But where should she start?

When things got tough, Jim Rockford always started by pulling his pistol out of the cookie jar. Then he hopped in his Firebird, shook down his informants and confronted the bad guys.

Lorraine didn't have a Firebird or any streetwise informants she could rough up, but she had something Rockford could have only dreamed about – a computer.

She cracked open Bernie's laptop and looked at the lock screen. What could his password be? Lorraine took a flier and typed in b-e-r-n-i-e-1. Bingo. No wonder this looked so easy on TV.

The browser history was incredibly dull, but one hundred percent Bernie. It showed every bowling blog in the history of ever, the homemade carbon fiber discussion board, a WebMD article about painful urination, search after search for "bowling tournament" and a Google maps destination for Wantagh, NY. She pulled up his Find My iPhone link and it dutifully tracked him to a diner on Sunrise Highway in Long Island, New York. Eat your heart out, Rockford.

Bernie wasn't exactly CIA material and Lorraine, a first-timer whose detective training consisted of watching every episode of The Mentalist, had tracked him down in the time it took to make a cup of herbal tea. And yet, she had not heard a peep from the police or the Wisco goons. The old Lorraine would have called the cops and handed over Bernie's computer. The new Lorraine knew that wouldn't get her anywhere. Time for Plan B.

She packed a bag, gassed up the Camry, programmed Wantagh into the GPS, reprogrammed the GPS because it wanted to take her to Wonton

City Chinese restaurant, reprogrammed the GPS again when it came up with One Ton Truck Center in Joplin, Missouri, then finally turned the stupid GPS off because it keep saying "recalculating" in a very disappointed and judgmental tone of voice.

Just in case there was trouble, she tried to remember a few of the moves she learned in the Tai Chi class she took at the city recreation center. And slipped the loaded Colt into her purse.

The gun was supposed to protect her from Bernie, but now it would have to protect Bernie. From what, she didn't know.

14

RAY ARRIVED AT THE VA holding a flannel shirt where his left ear used to be. It was soaked through and blood was dripping on the floor.

The charge nurse was not amused.

"Oh for Christ's sake, I just had that floor mopped," she said.

"If it's any consolation, I wiped my feet before I came in," Ray said.

"Don't be a smart mouth and stop bleeding on my floor."

"Sir, yes, sir."

"Take a seat before you pass out and hurt yourself."

Forty-five minutes later, the doctor got around to taking a look at Ray's missing ear and had a lot of questions.

Ray wasn't really in the mood for questions. After turning a murder into an attempted murder he was feeling pretty darn grouchy. And smoking was not allowed in the waiting room. Perfect.

"Sir, how did this happen?"

"I cut myself shaving."

"Seriously, sir, how did this happen?"

"What difference does it make? Just sew me up

and send me home."

"Sir, your injuries are consistent with a gunshot wound. I need to know what happened here."

The doctor had a point. Ray's face was covered with tiny black and red stipple marks from powder burns. He looked like the "before" guy in a zit cream commercial.

"It was a hunting accident."

"What happened?"

"Dick Cheney shot me. He hates me because I'm a Democrat.

"Seriously, please."

"He has terrible eyesight, maybe he thought I looked like a pheasant. I get that a lot."

"If I can't get a straight answer out of you, maybe the police can."

"Alright, alright. I was cleaning my shotgun, I thought it was unloaded, but, obviously, it wasn't. The thing blew up in my face and sprayed my ear all over the ceiling."

"Did you call the police?"

"I decided to come to the hospital before I bled to death."

"Good call. Way better than cleaning a loaded shotgun, by the way."

"Thanks for the safety tip, doc."

The VA is good at emergency medicine in general and trauma in particular. If you're hurt, they can patch you up quickly. VA doctors have seen things too gruesome to show up in your nightmares and they've brought back soldiers who would have long been given up for dead. They keep the fighting forces whole and, by extension, keep our country strong. While they're long on effectiveness, they are woefully short on style. The doctor stitched up the side of Ray's head leaving him with an earhole, part of an earlobe sticking straight out and whole bunch of stitches and bruises. He left the gunpowder burns alone.

"This won't hurt my ability to bowl, will it?," Ray said.

"No sir, you are medically cleared to bowl, but I'd recommend taking it easy for a couple of days, you've lost a lot of blood."

"No can do, have to go kick some ass in a tournament tomorrow."

"And you might want to double check that shotgun before you clean it again."

"Hey, while I'm here, can you check to see how I'm doing on the liver transplant list?"

"Not really."

"Okay, I'm on the list and I just have this feeling that a liver in my size is coming available very soon."

"I'm sure they'll let you know."

"Having no ear won't hurt my chances of getting a liver, will it?"

"They prefer patients who listen closely to their care instructions."

"Crap."

"I'm just kidding. You'll be able to hear fine and having an ear doesn't affect getting a liver."

"Just between you and me, if I find a liver on my own I can reserve it or something, right?"

"Where are you going to find a liver?"

"Around."

"Don't do that, sir."

"That's what's wrong with healthcare in this country."

With no gun, no shell casing, an uncooperative victim of a shovel attack and no real reason to even give a shit, the Nassau County police were only mildly interested in what happened behind the bowling alley. Besides, Tommy Hanrahan was on hand to head off any real questions.

"Hey Tommy," one of the other detectives said, "what do you think happened here?"

"Nickel and dime stuff. The guy who took the shovel to the head is a small time thug around town and he probably got crossways with some other small time thug who hit him in the head with the shovel. If it had been a big deal, we'd have the coroner out here."

"Yeah, but we ran the guy. He works part-time at Ikea and lives with his mother."

"Maybe he's with the Swedish mafia."

Tommy Hanrahan was one funny son of a bitch.

"What about this trail of blood, Tommy?"

"Looks like our boy got a shot in."

"With what? You see a gun or knife or anything? I don't."

"Who the hell knows with these guys? Maybe the other idiot took the weapon with him."

"It's a lot of blood, I'm gonna check the hospitals. Hey, you think Uncle Sally has a piece of this? There's something about that guy."

"What something?," Tommy said. "What's bothering you about Uncle Sally? The part where he's helping out the orphans or feeding the homeless on Thanksgiving? C'mon, if he spoke better Italian they'd make him the friggin' Pope."

"Yeah, you're probably right."

Tommy had no idea which mook left the long, wet trail of blood in the parking lot, but he did know he'd earned that month's pay. Time to get back to his real job.

"When you guys wrap this up," he said, "you want to grab a beer or three?"

The Crock Pot was having a tough time changing careers. The hit man thing started off a little bumpy and now had turned really bad. As he looked in the mirror at the crude staples holding his swollen face together, he could hear his mother sobbing in the background. It's times like this, he thought, that a weaker man would give up on his dreams.

He took stock of the situation.

It didn't look good.

His first hit took all night, turned into a big mess and got him stuck with a stupid nickname. Not ideal, but it was enough to get Uncle Sally to give him another shot.

His second hit has, so far, not gone according to plan. A random stranger hit him with a shovel, demolished his face and stole his shotgun. Crock Pot was hoping no one ever found out what happened to the sign. That wouldn't look good. And now he was banged up, wearing an eye patch and in competition with another hit man to see who could kill an unsuspecting bowler first.

This is not how it went in the movies.

Still, he knew he had a chance.

The regional bowling tournament was tomorrow. Leonard was never going to make it.

15

DEEP INSIDE the Wisco Bowling Security BOC (Bowling Observation Center), Mr. 221 was aggressively watching one of the regional finals for the Jani-San 100 Grand Whatever The Hell It Was Called bowling tournament.

One of the participants had already bowled a 280 and then a 300, which had triggered the BOC's automatic camera system. His third game in the series was looking just as strong. Mr. 221 brought up the camera hidden in the overhead scoring monitor above Lane 18, he had to put eyes on this superhuman bowler.

Then he wished he hadn't.

It was a short man about five foot five with a thin brown mustache and those prescription glasses that change color in the sun. The frames were out of style by a solid 20 years and, to be honest, they weren't that stylish back then. He was wearing a pair of pleated front Dockers a size too big and a threadbare golf shirt.

But capping it off was the piece de resistance, a giant poof of blonde hair that was so obviously a wig it was causing people to actually look away from the man. It wasn't a bad toupee, but a straight up wig. For a woman. From 1981. The hair was a shocking platinum blonde with feathered sides very much in the style Farrah Fawcett immortalized in the poster hung in the bedrooms of a generation of adolescent boys.

That wasn't the only thing that set him apart. His bowling technique was average at best. A reasonably good amateur, but nothing more. Kind of a soft looking four step approach, an arm swing that didn't really go back far enough to make the most of his clearly meager strength and a follow through that looked different every time.

On one throw he tried to put a little more power behind the ball and nearly toppled himself over the foul line. He looked like a 10-year-old throwing a 16-pound ball. But here's the kicker, it was a clean ball that hooked hard into the pocket for a strike.

With a few keystrokes Mr. 221 was into the bowling alley's point of sale computer system. The guy who signed up for the tournament and was now destroying pins on Lane 18 was named Sternie Beers.

What an idiot, Mr. 221 thought. I have found you and your magic bowling ball Bernie Steers. Your genius ass is mine.

The actions Mr. 221 should have taken at this point were clearly laid out in the Wisco Security Team Employee Handbook, which each member of the team was required to read and then eat upon completion. There were many items in the handbook, so it stands to reason that Mr. 221 could have forgotten one or two, but probably not the one about filing a report when the future of the game of bowling was on the line.

It was a fireable offense. The kind of firing that

ended with being sent to the bowling equivalent of Siberia: managing a bowling alley in the desolate wasteland of Odessa, Texas.

His other employer, Pinknockerz, would probably like to know about Mr. Steers' fine work, too. But Mr. 221 thought this discovery might earn him a little extra stipend above the five grand a month he was getting. Something on the order of, say, a million dollars. Pinknockerz might want to give him his own bowling alley or a Pinknockerz ball franchise, but he was holding out for two things. A million in cash and his name on the ball. His real name. Barney Steers.

Bernie Steers had never done an impulsive thing in his entire life. He was a go by the book kind of guy and it had served him well. He was doing the work he loved, had a wife who supported him, a daughter he didn't understand, the whole suburban American dream. Except one thing: respect.

As a child he was always regarded as a good bowler, but certainly not a great bowler. That spot was taken by his older brother, Barney. Bernie idolized his older brother. Tall, strong, handsome and an aggressive power bowler. Barney went away to college with a partial scholarship to bowling powerhouse South Dakota State University, where he became the first freshman ever to be named captain and went on to lead the team to one of their many NCAA bowling championships.

Then he vanished.

The police combed the South Dakota Badlands for his body. Nothing. They heard a rumor he had turned to the dark side and became a bowling hustler going from lane to lane sandbagging to get league bowlers to take him on for money, then turning on the jets and crushing them in front of their friends. Maybe one bet had gone too far and Barney paid the price.

What no one could ever know was that Barney was personally recruited to the Wisco Security Team. He had to cut all ties with friends and family and give his life to the protection of the game he loved. Barney did so with honor.

The stories about the bowling hustle were actually true. Barney was deep undercover to out an organized bowling gambling ring. Three Jamaican bowling con artists remain in jail to this day. Tax evasion landed them in prison, the bowling hustle got them a ticket.

Only one event gave Barney any pause. That was when his long lost brother joined Wisco as a junior engineer. He knew his brother had a brilliant mind for bowling, but never had the arm. Barney followed Bernie's career closely, even if it meant he had to live the rest of his life avoiding Bernie at the grocery store and post office in the suburban town they shared.

He knew Wisco would want Bernie and his ball. He also knew Bernie would never get the credit he deserved. This was Barney's chance to make everything right.

And make a million bucks at the same time.

Barney had spent a lot of time in the Wisco sub-sub basement.

When Bernie first pulled the BX300.9 out of the ball polisher, he could just feel it. The ninth try would be the winner. He felt a little like Dr. Frankenstein and had to work hard to stifle the urge to look up to the sky and scream, It's alive! It's alive!

But this bowling ball really was alive.

Inside, a set of lithium-ion batteries was powering a dizzying array of sensors, accelerometers and micro-sized hydraulic pumps to create a bowling ball that reconfigured itself a thousand times a second. It was his life's work and now it was ready to roll. Literally.

He carried the ball down to the Wisco test alleys. Designed to represent the different lanes bowlers might encounter, the test alleys were a study in bowling variables. Some were in pristine condition, some needed a lot of work. Some were so slick with oil a pro would struggle with them, others were dry as a bone.

Starting with the most average lane, Bernie took an easy swing, the ball missed the hook point and produced a tough 7-10 split. That was fine, Bernie thought, the computer inside the ball needed a few practice throws to learn the lane conditions and the bowler. He reset the pins and rolled again. He dropped all ten with ease.

Over the course of the afternoon he worked his way up and down the lanes. It took three throws for the ball to learn the toughest, pro level lanes. Then Bernie rolled two strikes in a row. He picked the ball up before he attracted too much attention.

His brother, Mr. 221, saw it all on his monitor.

There are things in a man's life he must do alone. Bernie knew that inside his bag was the bowling equivalent of a nuclear bomb. He could give it to his Wisco bosses to run with, but he worried they would destroy the game of bowling in the process.

Bernie was going to have to take a page from Bruce Springsteen and prove it all night. Not literally, he hoped, because he was usually in bed by nine-thirty.

The plan was simple and elegant. He would enter this huge, televised Jani-San Whatever Whatever bowling tournament and kick some serious ass. He would prove that, with the right equipment, brains could beat brawn. He would prove that he was the biggest thinker in the world of bowling ball engineering. He would prove he was successful. He would prove that Bernie Steers was a winner.

After winning the tournament at The Meadowlands he would dedicate his victory to the greatest bowler the world had never known. His brother, Barney Steers.

Of course, he'd have to do this in private. His family couldn't know, because this would be a dangerous adventure. There were people in the bowling world who would do anything to get their hands on this technology.

That's how Bernie Steers wound up winning a regional bowling tournament in a bowling alley a thousand miles from home disguised in a Farrah Fawcett wig. He sort of liked the long hair, it flowed on the approach and kind of floated when he settled into his follow through. Bernie thought it would look good on TV.

The Duval brothers liked the wig, too. Made Bernie a whole lot easier to find.

16

THE DUVAL BROTHERS TRIED HARD to blend in. Which was turning out to be pretty hard considering they were one black guy and one white guy driving around Long Island in a dirty white Ford pickup with a homemade flatbed constructed from old railroad ties and out of date Mississippi license plates that read BAMA SUX.

Sometimes you just have to work with what you've got.

And what they were working with right now was pretty sweet.

Not one, but two clients, had sent them to Long Island to look for bowlers. Two clients, on the same job! That Craig's List ad was really starting to pay off. They had ol' Dale from Jani-San who didn't want to pay out the prize money and wanted them to kidnap someone who could win the tournament and then give back the cash save for a little slice for themselves.

Jimmy and Timmy Duval had never actually kidnapped anybody, but they liked the idea of it.

Then they got a brand new client, some guy without a name, just a number like a secret agent. Mr. 221 wasn't a big conversationalist, but he did Western Union some money and that was all the conversation the Duvals needed. One way or another, this was going to be a score.

All they had to do was grab the guy in the wig.

Bernie collected his gear, stepped out of the bowling alley and climbed into his rented silver Kia Rio. He was trying to run this program on a budget.

The Duval brothers hopped into their trusty truck, which, of course, failed to start.

"Don't pump the gas, you'll flood it," Timmy said.

"Stupid truck."

"You just don't know what you're doing. If you keep cranking it you're gonna run down the battery."

"Get the starting fluid."

"Okay."

In order to have a really effective car chase you needed at least two cars. They were one short.

Timmy got the hood open and shot starting fluid into the carburetor. Jimmy hit the key and the engine garbled to some sense of life.

"What the hell is that sound?," Jimmy shouted over the knocking.

"It's a connecting rod going bad, been doing that for a couple of months."

"That sounds kinda serious, maybe we shoulda looked at that."

"Nah, it's fine."

It might have been fine for Mississippi, but it was struggling to get this New York car chase under way. Blue smoke was pouring from the exhaust and they were struggling to make forty miles an hour.

Fortunately, for them, they were chasing Bernie Steers. Sure, he had gone AWOL from his job, skipped out (temporarily) on his family and used a highly illegal, not to mention stolen, piece of equipment in a sanctioned bowling event, but Bernie was not one to break laws. He kept the Rio right at the local 30 mile per hour speed limit.

Inside the truck, things were getting louder and more than a little smoky.

"This thing doesn't sound so good," Jimmy said.

"Does it all the time," Timmy said.

Oil had begun to drip out of the engine and splashed on the ground in front of the rear tires causing the truck to slide around like a dirt track car. They swung wide around a minivan and clipped a newspaper box, which knocked them back into the middle of the street right behind Bernie's Kia as it was turning on to Sunrise Highway.

Bernie, knowing it was only a matter of time before someone found him, spotted them right away. He had made the highway and figured he could lose them there. Pressing the pedal to the floor made the engine get louder, but didn't make the car go much faster. 35, 40, 42. He had it floored, but that's all the little car would do.

Now that he thought about it, maybe he had the car a little bit overloaded. Former Eagle Scout that Bernie was, he had come prepared. For what, it was hard to say. The car was crammed with old bowling balls, trophies, medals, ribbons and boxes and boxes of bowling pins. Bernie figured he would hand them out during autograph sessions after winning the tournament. Doing a rough calculation behind the wheel of the wheezing rental, he figured he was about eighteen hundred pounds over the maximum recommended vehicle weight. That explained the gas mileage.

"Get out of the way, you moron," a mom

screamed from inside her minivan adding a nice, long horn honk as she swept around him in the fast lane.

By now, the truck had caught up. With smoke pouring out the back and a bad clatter under the hood, Jimmy had watched enough NASCAR to know the motor was about to let go. He had to get the deal done now.

Jimmy hammered the truck's gas pedal to the floor and slammed into Bernie's bumper. The overloaded hatchback swerved and Bernie managed to swing left, right and left again, but got it back under control. These guys were playing rough and Bernie had no idea what to do.

He decided to unload on them.

Bernie opened the window and started throwing out anything he could grab. The first bowling pin hit the bumper and rolled under the truck. With the second pin Bernie got lucky with a direct hit turning the truck's windshield into a spider web.

"Dammit," Jimmy said, "he's throwing crap at us and I can't see a thing."

He tossed an old 12-pound ball out the window. Bernie wasn't strong enough to toss it very high, so it fell harmlessly to the highway. Harmless until it rolled into the path of the truck's left front wheel. The old truck's suspension couldn't absorb driving over a bowling ball at 40 miles an hour resulting in a severely bent front wheel, a cracked king pin and a front suspension tie rod that looked like a snake on a three day bender. The truck was almost impossible to steer.

At the moment he ran over the ball, Jimmy was holding his head out the window so he could see around the shattered windshield. Launching an old Ford pickup three feet into the air was one thing, doing it while your head was hanging out the window was another move altogether. Jimmy's head clanged off the top of the truck's rusty door frame, down to the filthy windowsill and back up to the rusty doorframe opening up two nasty cuts on either side of Jimmy's head. If he had the time to think about it, he would have remembered his last tetanus shot was in 1983.

A man who knows how to stick to a plan, Bernie kept tossing things out the window.

Another bowling pin knocked out one of the truck's headlights. Then Bernie's hand fell to an old, three-foot tall bowling trophy. Out the window it went.

Jimmy, stunned after pinballing his skull all over the place, still had his head out the window. Thanks to the weird air currents flowing over the truck, caused mostly by the twelve-inch chrome plated hood ornament featuring a likeness of Ole Miss mascot "Colonel Reb" that the boys had installed ($19.99 at AutoZone), the trophy flipped around flying marble base first and landing squarely on the bridge of Jimmy's nose. The cartilage immediately turned to jelly and his eyes started to swell shut. Now he was bleeding from three places on his head. And he couldn't see a thing.

Timmy grabbed the wheel.

Calling Sunrise Highway a highway is sort of a local euphemism. A highway, in most parts of the country, is an elevated road where you drive more or less unabated to your destination which is reached by use of an exit ramp.

Sunrise Highway is nothing like that.

It has stoplights. Yes, stoplights. On a highway.

Sunrise Highway traffic moving at 55 miles an hour is expected to come to an orderly stop in order to let other traffic cross. You don't have to be a traffic engineer to see this is a high speed demolition derby waiting to happen.

Bernie saw the light turn yellow. He probably could have made it, but that wasn't how Bernie drove. Just as he was instructed to in tenth grade driver's ed, he applied the brakes firmly and came to a complete and controlled stop. Behind him, things were a little different.

By now the truck's cab had filled with acrid smoke and the stench of human blood. Timmy was in the passenger seat using his left hand to saw at the wheel, which really wasn't having much effect thanks to the heavily damaged suspension and bent front wheel. Jimmy, in the driver's seat, was dividing his time between flooring the gas and bleeding.

Timmy was working hard to keep the truck on the highway when he saw the Kia's brake lights come on and the car he was trying to catch started getting very close, very fast. Timmy reacted and swung the wheel. He had two choices, left or right. He chose right. Which means he chose wrong.

The four members of the Steamfitters Union Local 638 were on their way home from a hard day of steamfitting after a quick stop to purchase four 16-ounce Natural Light beers cleverly concealed in brown paper bags. No one ever drank anything but beer from brown paper bags, but it was a ruse that made the drinker feel like he'd at least made some kind of effort at subterfuge.

Beers in hand and five o'clock behind them, the steamfitters were ready to unwind. That's when the

Duvals unwound right into them.

According to police reports, the event was listed as part traffic accident, part domestic disturbance. The crash was caused by a truck with expired Mississippi plates driven by either James or Timothy Duval of Jackson, Mississippi, slamming into a full size van owned and driven by Vito Nicolito with three of his friends inside. While toxicology reports are still pending, police believe alcohol may have been a factor due to the presence of beer cans hidden in brown paper bags found at the scene.

After the accident, witnesses said all six men climbed from the two demolished vehicles displaying a wide variety of injuries. The driver of the pickup had several facial lacerations and a broken leg. Through a broken jaw he kept telling police, "bowling trophy." He was taken away for psychiatric observation.

The second passenger in the pickup, Timothy Duval, also suffered serious injuries. Colliding with the van caused the truck's dying engine to explode and sent a brief flash of fire through the cabin. This was just enough to ignite the can of starting fluid held between Timothy's legs. His groin in flames, he staggered out of the truck. Vito and his traveling companions put out the flames by kicking and stomping Mr. Duval causing facial injuries and several broken ribs to go along with the second and third degree crotch burns.

The steamfitters were treated for minor abrasions, given signed medical authorizations entitling them to four weeks of paid time off, and released.

From Bernie's point of view the crash was horrific. Screeching tires, breaking glass, creaking metal. Bernie assumed that New York State law would compel him to stop and render aid, but he decided to make an exception in this case, since the accident victims were clearly trying to kill him. He gunned the Kia and limped off into the night.

What Bernie didn't see was the car to his left, an old Dodge Neon with a young couple inside. The woman in the passenger seat looked over just before the accident.

She looked at the driver and said, "Look, in that car, I could swear that's my dad."

"In the Farrah Fawcett wig?"

"I'm telling you, it's him."

Then came the crash, the explosion and the man in the wig was gone.

Dealing with a car crash, an explosion and a brawl explains why the Nassau County police failed to notice the man and woman in identical black business suits step out of the black Suburban with Wisconsin plates. They were picking up pieces of a bowling ball from the gutter.

"What do you see, 176?"

"Looks like a piece of a broken bowling ball."

"No shit, genius. Look at the ball."

"Looks pretty normal to me."

"Exactly. It's just a normal rental grade ball. The ball we're looking for is still out there."

17

"ARE YOU MY CONTACT?," asked Mr. 221.

"No, I'm just a random creepy guy who sits next to strange men on park benches. And why the hell are we meeting on a park bench? The whole thing is like a bad spy movie."

"What's your name?"

"Franklin Roosevelt."

"What happened, was Thomas Jefferson busy? That's the worst code name ever."

"My mother didn't think so when she put it on my birth certificate. What am I supposed to call you, besides jackass?"

"221."

"Are you serious? I can't even respond to that."

Franklin Roosevelt wasn't part of the Pinknockerz Security Team, he was the team. Trained in subterfuge and demolition, courtesy of your United States Army, Roosevelt's true calling was the sartorial arts. While Mr. 221 showed up in the standard Wisco issue black suit/white shirt/black tie combo, Roosevelt was resplendent in a bespoke five-button suit, lavender shirt with matching tie, diamond stickpin, shoulder length dreadlocks and a pair of wraparound sunglasses. The only thing that even hinted at his career as a bowling security expert were the solid gold cufflinks made from a pair of 300 perfect game rings.

"You don't exactly look like a bowler," said 221.

"And you don't exactly look smart. Stop wasting my time. Why am I here?"

"I need a new deal."

"Listen, we pay you five grand a month. For nothing, as far as I'm concerned."

"I've sent plenty of useful information your way."

"So has Google and we don't pay them 60 grand a year."

"What if I told you there was a new ball out there. A ball that could change the game forever. Literally a game changer."

"We know all about your magic bowling ball. When somebody sneezes at your place I catch a cold."

"But you don't have the ball and I do."

"Bullshit."

"I'll have it soon."

"Okay, I'll bite. What do you want?"

"I want to use it to run Pinknockerz out of business, but that's above my pay grade."

"And you think you can score a big payday with me."

"A million dollars," 221 said dramatically.

"Fine. Deal."

"That was a little too easy."

"Because I think there's a zero percent chance that your dumb cracker ass actually gets that ball. My million dollars will still be resting comfortably in its interest-bearing municipal bonds account."

"I will get that ball."

"Not if I get it first."

Both men were suppressing very strong urges to kill the other. 221 was quite confident he could reach up with both hands and snap Franklin Roosevelt's neck and Franklin was visualizing how he would stab 221 through the eye socket with the arm of his carbon fiber sunglasses.

"A million dollars for the ball."

"I can't believe I had to come all the way to East Buttcrack, Wisconsin for this. You could have sent me an e-mail."

"The e in e-mail stands for evidence, Mr. Roosevelt. We're talking about corporate espionage."

"We're talking about a bowling ball. Fun fact, Mr. Number Instead of a Name: no one gives a crap. And is there anywhere in this freak show of a town where I can get a decent shoeshine and some sushi?"

This is a hard way to make a million dollars, thought Mr. 221.

What an self-righteous asshole, thought Mr. Roosevelt.

18

TURNS OUT KILLING PEOPLE was way harder than it looked on TV. Ray's first crack at being a cold blooded killer wound up with him getting his ear shot off and having to answer a lot of questions at the VA emergency room. He wasn't sure which was more painful. At least he got a snappy looking camouflage shotgun out of the deal.

Ray might just have to win this bowling tournament fair and square. That plan sucked, but it was the only one he had.

Earlier in the week he had played in the Centereach Lanes O'Fun regional tournament as a warm up. Ray didn't try that hard, because the bowlers in Centereach could barely walk without scraping their knuckles on the ground. He spent most of the time drinking beer, smoking cigs and eating hot dogs. In the last frame, he didn't even bother putting his beer down. He still came in as the first alternate. Ray didn't want to get in to the tournament that way, he wanted to beat real bowlers like the guys in Massapequa. And that's what was on the agenda for today.

Of course, if Ray screwed up and didn't win at Massapequa, he figured he could just go kill the guy on the list in front of him. Now that he knew how not to do it.

Ray Flanagan did not consider himself a professional athlete. He was much better than that. Ray thought those NFL and NBA guys were soft. Riding around in Escalades, getting pedicures, having trainers rub them down with aromatherapy oils at halftime. Primped, pampered pussies every one.

That's not how real men went about their business and definitely not how Ray went about his. Today was game day and Ray had a time-honored routine that never let him down.

Get up at 6:30 a.m., meet the day head-on with a quick eye-opener in the form of a shot of whiskey or rye, whatever was handy, and a nice, relaxing cigarette.

Next, a shower and some coughing. A shave and a little more coughing. Finally, get dressed and get ready to go.

Now it was time for breakfast. That meant the diner down the street where Ray would order three eggs over, three pieces of bacon, a slice of ham, a stack of pancakes (carbo loading) and a bottomless cup of coffee. The last cup in the traditional Irish fashion.

Arriving at the bowling alley he would pay his money and begin the last phase of his warm up routine. Ray would bend over at the waist and put on his left bowling shoe then bend over again to put on his right shoe. This would have the double effect of stretching him out and putting on his shoes. Big time saver. Finally, he'd ask Sheila to bring him a shot of Jack with two beers back and then off to the men's room for a last minute pee and to vomit up some blood. The vomiting of blood had become an important of Ray's warm up routine. It made him feel tough, invincible. Sure, he was dying, but he was still in the game. Let's see Tom Brady work dying into his warm up routine. The vomiting might mess up his hair.

"Sheila, bring me the usual before we get rolling here," Ray said.

"What happened to your face, honey?"

Ray was sporting a bandage that covered the whole side of his head. It had a growing red stain where his ear used to be. Damn thing wouldn't stop bleeding.

"Cut myself shaving. I could really use a drink or three."

"Love to, honey, but it's against the rules today."

"Rules? What the hell are you talking about?"

"Leonard says this is an official tournament, rule book, governing body, spirit of the game, blah, blah, blah, so there's no drinking or smoking. There might be impressionable children watching."

"Impressionable children? That's what fucking bumper bowling is for. This is a real grown up sport."

"My stars, with all these reporters here I could use a drink, but rules are rules, hon."

Ray stomped off to confront his nemesis.

He found Leonard in the pro shop and jammed him up against what was left of the ball drilling machine to have a few words with him. Ray was really fighting the urge to shove Leonard's head under there and crank it up.

"What the fuck, Leonard?"

"What happened to your face, Ray?"

"The same thing that's going to happen to yours if I don't get a drink pretty soon."

"We're having an official tournament, Ray, we're

going by the PBA rulebook today. No drinking, no smoking. Could be kids in the audience."

Ray leaned in a little harder.

"I've been drinking at this bowling alley since you were crapping your pants. Now, suddenly, it's no drinking? And what's with the smoking? I have a Constitutional right to smoke in a bowling alley, this is the United States of America, you know."

Leonard was no Constitutional scholar, but he was pretty sure smoking in bowling alleys was not covered in the Bill of Rights.

"Listen, you little prick, get me a Jack and Coke right now, or I'm going to talk to Al."

"Knock yourself out."

Ray stomped off to find Al. He didn't have to stomp far, because Al was in the bar. Having a drink.

"Al, the kid says I can't have drinks or smokes on the lanes. Tournament rules or some crap like that. Bullshit, right?"

Hoping that Leonard would have been long dead by now, Al wasn't interested in getting involved.

"It's the kid's tournament, he can do what he wants."

"Listen Al, I gotta win this thing today and I only bowl my best when I have a couple of frosty cold ones and a Marlboro menthol with me."

"This is about your performance in today's bowling tournament, right?"

"Thanks Al, you know what I'm talking about."

"Ray, what makes you think I give two shits about anything to do with bowling? News flash: I don't. So either shut up and bowl or get the fuck out. I don't care which as long as it doesn't involve me."

"I thought we were friends."

"I'll send you a Christmas card, dick face."

Ray had only a few minutes to get ready so he stomped out to his truck for a quick smoke and a long pull off the emergency bottle of Wild Turkey he kept stashed in the glove compartment. People and reporters were streaming past him going into the bowling alley, but no one seemed to take notice of the dried blood drips down the side of Ray's truck and the rather large bloody handprint on the door. Of course, when you live in Nassau County, you seen one bloody handprint, you seen 'em all.

"Very funny, sir, but no," said the regional PBA official in charge of the tournament.

Bowling tournaments didn't routinely draw much press, but since this one was taking place at the site of the great Zamboni Shoot Out and Triple Murder Mayhem, there were quite a few cameras around. Attendance by the press tended to bring out the wackos and today was no different. A man was standing in front of the entry table with his chimpanzee, Mr. Sprinkles, trying to enter the beast into the event. To be fair, Mr. Sprinkles really looked the part. He had a bowling bag, a bowling shirt with his name stitched over the pocket, three-tone bowling shoes, a Winston hanging out of his mouth and he was carrying a six pack of Bud. If he had been a little taller he would have been in, no questions asked.

"And, by the way, no smoking during an official tournament."

The chimp dutifully spit the Winston out.

"Listen," the man with the chimp said, "Mr.

Sprinkles is a hell of a bowler. I've been through the PBA rulebook a thousand times and there's nothing in there that says you have to be of any certain species to participate."

"Isn't that just kind of assumed?"

"Excuse me," said a large man in a tailored pinstriped suit and carrying a briefcase. "I represent Mr. Sprinkles in all legal matters and this gentleman is correct, the PBA rulebook does not explicitly rule out pan troglodytes, otherwise known as chimpanzees, from participating in officially sanctioned bowling contests."

"Okay, I get it, where are the hidden cameras?"

"This isn't a joke, sir, I have a judge standing by to issue a restraining order to shut down these proceedings if my client is not permitted to participate."

"If he doesn't have any ID, I can't let him in. My hands are tied."

The man with the chimp produced a valid New York driver's license with the chimp's photo and bearing the name Sprinkles Morgenstern.

"You should see him parallel park. It's a gift."

"Good enough for me."

Mr. Sprinkles was in. His first round opponent: Ray Flanagan.

For being bow-legged and having opposable thumbs for big toes, Mr. Sprinkles had pretty decent footwork. He'd switch from a four step approach to a five step approach to sometimes just standing on the line and letting it rip.

You couldn't question his arm swing or his raw strength, but it was his hands that really made the difference. His fingers were much farther apart than a human's, so when he spun the ball it rotated like crazy. You could hear Mr. Sprinkles' multi-colored ball hook into the pocket from next door.

That monkey could bowl.

Ray had never been more pissed in his life. He roared at the PBA official about the monkey. And when he didn't make any progress about the monkey, he started in on the prohibition of drinking and smoking.

"If it's any consolation," the PBA official said, "I told the monkey he couldn't smoke, either."

"How can you let a goddamn monkey into a bowling tournament? Aren't all the players supposed to be able to at least walk upright?"

"I've been to a lot of bowling tournaments, sir, and that's not always the case."

All this conflict was not good for what was left of Ray's health. The fact that his liver was starting to fail had turned his eyes a glowing yellow and gave his skin a waxy, tallow look. This morning's bandage over the side of his face was already soaked through with blood. Ray had raided the bowling alley's first aid kit and applied every single item on top of what was already there. He was like a living bandage catalog. There were butterflies, strips of gauze, pads, squares, traditional bandages of all sizes, even 15 of those little dots you use when you cut yourself shaving. Ray may have been losing the battle, but the bandages were fighting their little adhesive hearts out.

It only got worse when the game started. Sprinkles was getting inside Ray's head, jumping up and down on top of the ball return and screaming every time he threw a strike. The crowd was going crazy. After all, when it was a bloody, limping old man versus a super cute monkey in a tiny bowling shirt, who were they going to pull for?

Ray couldn't get focused, his bowling was erratic, he was barely staying ahead of Mr. Sprinkles. If Ray didn't start throwing strikes soon, he was in danger of getting beat by a primate. A fellow primate, technically.

Going into the tenth, Ray's prayers were answered. Not exactly, because Ray had not been praying and, in fact, had not prayed since the night before a big algebra test the year his mother made him go to Our Lady of Eternal Sorrows Catholic School. Whether it was divine intervention or not, Ray would never know and, honestly, would never care.

Sometimes the smallest things make a difference and this time it was a fun size Baby Ruth bar. It was a chilly day and 9-year-old Larry Brigand was wearing his coat. Mostly because his mother made him. The last time she made him wear it was on Halloween. He casually reached into the pocket and was thrilled to find a fun size Baby Ruth bar that he had left in the pocket. Larry took it out and unwrapped it. The bar was a little bit crushed and over the months had grown kind of gray around the edges, but for a 9-year-old stuck at a boring bowling tournament it was a fantastic treasure.

He never saw the monkey.

What little Larry could never have known was that Baby Ruth bars were the very special treat used to train Mr. Sprinkles ever since he was a little chimp. He'd do anything for a Baby Ruth bar. He was jumping up and down on the ball return waiting for his ball to come back when he heard the telltale sound of the wrapper tearing.

In a split second, he leaped on to Ray's head, pushed off him to jump into the third row, climbed over heads and arms and shoulders until he got to the boy. He promptly took the boy's candy bar, bit him on the arm and ran out of the building.

Ray won by forfeit. He'd drink to that. Sooner the better.

19

SOMETIMES YOU HAVE TO IMPROVISE. When you're a junior hit man who lost his gun, you definitely fall into this category.

Sally the Crock Pot was ready. After Googling "how to burn down a house," he arrived at a plan. He would get to Leonard's house before dawn and torch the place with Leonard in it. The job would be done before breakfast. Which was good because Crock Pot was starving.

First he had to go shopping. He bought a few five-gallon gasoline jugs, a bag of rags and some paint thinner. From there he went to the gas station, filled up the jugs and bought a disposable lighter.

The trouble with improvisation is that there really isn't time to work out the details. Like, will a bunch of five-gallon jugs filled with gasoline fit in the trunk of a Chevy Cavalier? The answer, it turns out, is no. The Crock Pot seat belted two of the jugs into the back seat and the third into the passenger seat. Next stop, 108 Clark Street.

He parked and started to unload his supplies.

Five-gallon gas cans are much heavier than they look. Crock Pot, still feeling pretty sore from being hit in the head with a shovel, got the first can out of the front bucket seat, but was really struggling to drag the other two out of the back seat. One more hard tug and the last one came out of the car splashing a good quart of gasoline all over the Crock Pot's sport coat. (He felt it was important to always dress for success.) He flailed for the jug and caught it in a big bear hug only to feel a slight twinge in his back and feel his legs fold up.

Down went the Crock Pot. Doctors would say later that it was a particular combination of a bulging disk and too much lasagna that caused the nerve to pinch and switch his legs into the off position.

The casual observer would have assumed the Crock Pot was a trained military demolition expert instead of a guy with a back spasm. He was belly crawling around the house dragging cans of gasoline behind him. Periodically, he'd stop and shove a gasoline-soaked rag into the spaces underneath the doors and windows. Sometimes he would just lay there and catch his breath.

The newspaper delivery guy drove by and saw the aspiring hit man laying in the yard. Nothing new, he thought, just another drunk who couldn't quite crawl to the door.

Crock Pot dragged the half empty gas cans to the car, threw them in, then dragged himself up off the ground by hanging on to the car's open door. He held up one of the gasoline soaked rags, lit it with the disposable lighter and got ready to watch his hard work come together.

Fire isn't particular, it will burn whatever is the most appetizing fuel available. Including the gas that had soaked into the Crock Pot's left pants leg and sleeve of his sport coat. He whipped off the flaming sport coat (he was really pissed because he had just bought that coat last year during the buy one get one free Joseph A. Bank Dads and Grads sale) and used it to beat out the flames on his pants, but not before he was wearing an interesting pair of sansabelt culottes.

During the pants extinguishing process a lick of flame leaped off the sport coat and found the trail leading back to the cans inside the Cavalier which lit up the car's interior immediately. Flapping the sport coat on the burning car seats sent shooting pains through his lower back and leg which distracted him from the burn pains a little. Crock Pot failed to notice that at least one part of his plan went right.

The house at 108 Clark Street was going up in flames.

Flickering firelight framed the For Sale sign beautifully.

Meanwhile, over at 104 Clark Street, Leonard was rousted out of a sound sleep by fire trucks racing to the blaze at the neighbor's house. The Russos had put the house up for sale when they moved to Texas. Neighbors said they were six months behind on the mortgage and now it was on fire. Funny how that worked out, Leonard thought. Since he was up, he took a shower, ate some breakfast and made his way over to the Pin and Pub.

Leonard was feeling good, his game was solid, he knew these lanes better than any man alive and, most of all, he knew the competition. Except for the monkey, that was a total surprise.

He bowled through the early rounds, the

quarterfinals and faced a tough competitor in the semis, but was able to grind his way through.

Leonard had made the regional finals.

"I'm proud of you Leonard," Susie said. "You didn't get beat by the monkey."

"Hey, that monkey has a mean hook."

"But having four hands really hurts your footwork."

"I'm up against Ray in the final."

"Seriously? The guy who almost lost to the monkey?"

"Yeah, but he's a really good bowler, very tough when he's on his game."

Currently, what Ray was on was his knees. Vomiting up blood.

The day had been pretty tough on Ray. For starters, his blood alcohol level was a lot lower than he was used to. Even though he was grabbing quick smokes in the parking lot between matches, he was suffering from some kind of nicotine withdrawal and because his stupid liver was on its farewell tour, his shot off ear wouldn't stop bleeding. Vomiting blood seemed to be the least of his problems.

One of the regulars came into the men's room.

"Hey Ray," the guy said, "looks like you got Leonard in the final. Kick his ass, Ray."

Ray signaled his thanks by tossing some more bright red chunks.

"And now, Massapequa Pin and Pub presents," the announcer said into the microphone, "the last match in the regional finals of the Jani-San 100 Grand, er uh, what is it again...presented by Scratch-Eze Antifungal Spray Bowling Tournament! Ray Flanagan versus Leonard Fleischman."

The crowd applauded. Louder than a golf clap, but not much.

"Mr. Flanagan won the coin flip and he will bowl first. Let's get ready to roooooollllllllll!"

Leonard believed bowling was a sport of manners, etiquette and civility. So he stepped over to Ray, stuck out his right hand with the wrist guard and said, "Good luck."

"Fuck you," came the reply.

Ray was focused. Mostly. He could see the ball clearly, the pins were all there, it was just the edges that were fuzzy. He stepped up to the ball rack, lifted up his trusty 16-pounder and let it rest in front of his chest. Slowly, he leaned forward staring down the ten pins at the end of the lane. He could feel the blood start to drip down his cheek, but he didn't care, because he was in the zone.

Then he was on the floor.

Leonard didn't want a free pass to The Meadowlands, but he'd take it. If that meant accepting a forfeit from a guy he really didn't like that much, fine.

"Nice bowling, champ," Susie said.

"It's all in the wrist," Leonard said.

While the paramedics worked on Ray, Leonard took a second to look out over the crowd. Not the usual folks you'd expect to see at Massapequa Pin and Pub. There was the guy who worked for Uncle Sally, the Crock Pot they called him, hunched over a chair looking like he'd just seen a ghost. Leonard realized he was the guy they had seen in the alley after getting hit with a shovel. Only now he looked even worse. Half his hair and both eyebrows were burned off, he was wearing an eye patch, one sleeve of his sport coat was missing and his pants had been singed up to capri length.

Then there was a pair of guys who looked like they'd just got back from an ultimate fighting fantasy camp. The white man had his eyes nearly swollen shut, a huge bandage on his nose and his arm in a sling. The black man next to him had a swollen nose, swollen jaw, a neck brace and looked like his pants had been cut off and then stuck back together with medical tape.

In the back were two solemn figures, a man and a woman dressed in matching black business suits with very noticeable bulges underneath their left arms. And slipping out the side door was the man in the Farrah Fawcett wig.

20

BERNIE STEERS WAS IMPRESSED with the competition. Leonard Fleischman was a good young bowler. It would make Bernie sad to crush him with the BX300.9, but as they said in the mob movies, it wasn't personal, it was business. What complicated things even more was that his daughter was here with Leonard. How had she found him? Damn internet, he thought.

Right after the big guy who was bleeding profusely from the side of his head passed out, Bernie turned for the door. Although he felt really confident about the effectiveness of his wig disguise, he had to get out of there before his daughter got too close. If she found him, his plan would be in serious jeopardy.

He never saw the monkey.

Sprinkles Morgenstern, still on a sugar high from the Baby Ruth bar, swung down from the awning and grabbed for the wig. Bernie wasn't about to give up the hair without a fight, he paid thirty eight dollars plus tax at the wig shop and had to tangle with a drag queen named Silky Bear.

"That wig doesn't suit you, honey," Silky Bear said. "Let me have it."

"I need it."

"Why don't you pick one of these other wigs? And what kind of drag queen has a mustache? You need to wax that thing, baby."

Bernie gave the wig a big tug, marched up to the counter and paid. With his credit card.

Now he was fighting off a monkey in a tiny bowling shirt. And losing.

"Let the monkey have the wig, Dad."

Stunned, Bernie whirled around to see his daughter, Susie. He remembered the day she was born and they named her after Earl Anthony's beloved wife.

He dropped his hands and let the monkey have the wig. It actually looked pretty good on the chimp, really accentuated his eyes.

"What are you doing here, Dad? Mom is worried sick and I've been tracking you halfway across the country."

"How did you find me?"

"You used your credit card to rent a car."

"Dang, forgot."

"And to buy gas in Indiana, Ohio, Pennsylvania and New York."

"I had to buy gas."

"You used it to buy some gum here at the bowling alley, I saw you. Who puts gum on a credit card?"

"I meant to press debit. You spotted me with the wig?"

"Let's just forget the wig ever happened, okay? What's going on, Dad?"

"I'm sorry, dear, it's really complicated, you see there's this bowling ball and I've been feeling kind of weird lately and..."

"Nice to meet you, Mr. Steers, I'm Leonard

Fleischman."

"Steers and Fleischman, just the two guys we've been looking for," said Jimmy Duval who stepped around the corner holding a rusty old revolver.

"What?"

Jimmy's mouth was wired shut making him difficult to understand.

"We've been looking for y'all," Timmy Duval said.

"We're here to kidnap all of you," Jimmy said.

"What? You're mumbling."

"He said, we're here to kidnap you, so come on."

"I don't think this is how you kidnap someone," Susie said. "You can't just stand there and say, 'come on, you're kidnapped.'"

"The gun should help," Jimmy said.

"Seriously, you are going to have to speak up."

"We've got guns and the guns do the talking," Timmy said.

"It's logical," Bernie said.

"So you guys are officially kidnapped," Timmy said, "Whoo-hoo!" He turned and high fived his brother on their very first successful kidnapping.

The little group stood there for a few seconds staring at each other and trying to figure out what to do next.

"What are we supposed to do now?," Leonard said.

"I'm getting hungry," Susie said.

"Good idea, we should get something to eat," Bernie said.

"Hold on a second, we're the kidnappers, we make the rules," Jimmy said.

"Yeah," Timmy said.

"I still can't understand a word he's saying," Bernie

said.

Kidnapping people was a lot harder than the Duval brothers thought.

"We need a car," Timmy said.

"We'll just hot wire one," Jimmy said.

Jimmy took the butt of the pistol and bashed it against the window of the nearest car. Nothing. He hit harder. Still nothing. Timmy reached over and tried the door. Open.

Jimmy climbed in, fished some wires out from under the dashboard and tried rubbing them together. Then he tried a couple of other wires. If he'd had a schematic diagram of a Honda Accord and the knowledge to read it, he would have known that touching the stereo wire to the cigarette lighter wire was not going to start the car.

"We could just take my car," said Leonard.

"Give me your keys," Jimmy said.

Jimmy shoved the pistol in his waistband and hopped in the driver's seat as Leonard briefed him on the idiosyncrasies of the Neon.

"You kind of have to goose the gas pedal at traffic lights to keep it from stalling," Leonard said. "And jiggle the ignition key if it gets stuck."

"What the fuck is this?"

"What?"

"Is this a stick shift?"

"You don't know how to drive a stick?" The entire group stopped and looked at Jimmy who saw this as a direct affront to his manhood.

"Hell yes, of course I know how to drive a stick, I grew up driving a stick. Timmy can back me up on that."

"Huh," Timmy offered in the way of backup.

"You'd better drive since you know the area and I can keep you covered."

"What should we do with our balls?", Bernie asked.

The Duval brothers giggled instinctively at the mention of the word "balls."

"Whatever, put them in the trunk."

"I'd rather keep my balls with me," Bernie said.

They cracked up again.

"Why not, I always keep mine with me," Timmy said, causing both Duvals to double over with laughter. Jimmy had to put a hand on the car to keep from falling down.

The bowlers failed to get the joke and crammed in the car.

Leonard drove and Jimmy took the front passenger seat so he could wave the rusty revolver around. Bernie, Susie, Timmy and three bowling ball bags were jammed into the back seat.

"Seat belts everyone," Leonard called out. Which set off an uncomfortable game of Twister while everyone found seat belts buried in the seat cushions and then buckled themselves in. Safety first. Even in a kidnapping.

"What happened to your pants?," Susie asked Timmy.

"They got cut off in the emergency room and I had to tape them back together."

"Why were you in the emergency room and, more important, why do you only have one pair of pants? Total cut-rate kidnapping. This sucks. Seriously, have you guys ever kidnapped anyone before?"

"Sure, lots of times," Jimmy mumbled.

"Yeah, lots of times," Timmy agreed.

"You have not."

"Have, too."

"Have not."

"Have, too."

"Knock it off, you guys," Leonard said, "Or I'll turn this car around and go straight back to the bowling alley."

"I think everyone's just hungry," Bernie said.

"This is the worst kidnapping ever!," Susie said.

"Everybody just shut up!," Jimmy said.

Jimmy and Timmy's first kidnapping was off to a rocky start, but at least it was going. Time to dial for dollars.

"Hello, this is Dale Saxby."

"Hey Dale, it's Timmy."

Dale wilted a little. He got the dumb one.

"Where's Jimmy?"

"He's right here. His jaw's wired shut."

"I don't even want to know."

"We got your bowling tournament winner right here."

"For some reason, I'm counting on you."

"Let's talk money."

"There's nothing to talk about Timmy."

"We've run into a lot of unforeseen expenses. Doctor bills. Tape for my pants. I'm saving my receipts."

"The deal is the deal, Timmy."

"C'mon, Dale."

"If you try to screw me on this, Timmy, I will shove your body into a 55 gallon drum of cleaning fluid. It'll be a real nice smelling funeral."

Click.

Taking a carload of toddlers with ADHD through a fast food drive-thru would be bad, but the Duval brothers would have preferred it to this group.

"May I take your order, please?," garbled the speaker.

"What do they have?," asked Susie.

"What do they have?," said Jimmy. "It's McDonald's, they have the same stuff they've had for 50 fucking years! Hamburgers, french fries, shakes."

"Oooh, can we get shakes?," Timmy asked. "Strawberry for me."

"May I take your order?"

"Just a second, please," Leonard said.

"Everybody just shut up and let me think," Jimmy growled.

"He has to think about what to order at McDonald's?," Bernie whispered to Susie. "First timers, for sure."

"Okay, okay," Jimmy took a deep breath. "Let's order."

"We're ready," Leonard said.

"Five hamburgers..."

Leonard repeated the order to the little speaker, "Five hamburgers..."

"Can I have a cheeseburger?," Susie said.

"Five cheeseburgers," Jimmy said through gritted teeth. "Five small fries, five small Cokes."

"Five cheeseburgers," Leonard started.

"I can't eat a cheeseburger," said Timmy.

"What?"

"I'm lactose intolerant."

"Then, what do you want?"

"Strawberry shake."

"Fine, four cheeseburgers, one hamburger, five small fries, four small Cokes and one strawberry shake."

"Okay, four cheese..."

"Hey, how come he gets to have a shake and I don't?," said Susie.

"Because you're the one being kidnapped," said Jimmy.

"Excuse me?," came the voice over the speaker.

"Nothing," said Leonard.

"Pull around to the window, please."

Jimmy slid the gun under him and Leonard drove up to the window.

"That'll be $23.37."

Nobody moved.

Leonard looked at Jimmy, "Well?"

"Well, what? Pay her."

"Are you kidding me?," Susie went off. "You kidnap him and then you want him to buy his own lunch? That's it, I am out of here."

She opened the door, grabbed the bowling bag and got out.

"When you're ready to do some real kidnapping, let me know."

Susie slammed the door and stomped off.

Jimmy looked at the woman in the drive through window who was stunned by the entire scene. "Is it too late to change my order?"

Back on the road with everyone eating a little lunch and not talking, Jimmy figured he'd take a run at Mr. 221.

"Yes?," Mr. 221 said.

"It's Jimmy Duval."

"That's good to say your name nice and clear so the authorities, who are no doubt listening to this call, can hear you. Probably want to go ahead and let them know what you'd like to have for your last meal. That would be a big time saver."

"We gotta talk."

Mr. 221 lived his entire adult life in the shadows dealing with scum like Jimmy Duval. He knew this call was coming.

"We've got the goods," Jimmy hissed into the phone.

"What the hell is that supposed to mean, you country idiot?"

"I was speaking in code."

"Try speaking in English for a change. And stop mumbling."

"We've kidnapped..."

"Hold it right there, Lil Abner. Kidnapping is a crime and certainly not a thing I would be talking about with a known criminal on an unsecured cellular telephone line."

"Um."

"Perhaps you meant 'acquired?'"

"Yeah, yeah, that's what I meant," Jimmy said. Then to Timmy he said, "This guy is a major league pain in the ass."

"What was that?"

"Nothing, we have acquired Bernie Steers, Leonard Fleischman and Fleischman's girlfriend. Skip that last part, we don't have the girlfriend anymore, she left."

Leonard focused on the word "girlfriend."

"Do you have the ball?"

"They all have balls."

Both Duvals giggled.

"What does it say on it?"

"It says, I and a picture of a heart and then my local public television station."

"Not the bag, you moron. What does it say on the ball?"

"It's got a name on it."

"Read it to me."

"It says pink knockers."

"You mean, Pinknockerz?"

"Yeah, that's it. Gotta be worth another ten grand."

"It's not worth ten cents. You got the wrong ball, shit for brains. Without that ball, you're not getting a dime."

"Uh, speaking of money, we've, uh, run into, er, a few additional expenses and we..."

"You want more money."

"Yeah, that's it. We're going to need more money."

"And I need my bowling ball."

"Okay."

"You have Fleischman and Steers?"

"Yep."

"Kill Fleischman, bring me Steers."

"You shouldn't be saying that over an unsecured cell phone line."

"Do what I say or there won't be enough left of you to fill a corn cob pipe."

Click.

Jimmy really wished he hadn't made that call. He also wished Leonard would stop making the car jerk back and forth.

"What are you doing?," Jimmy yelled at Leonard.

"Running out of gas," said Leonard as he quietly pressed the send button on his phone to text the word "help" to the only person who could save him now.

Jimmy Duval looked down at his own ringing phone to see who was calling. A number from Shreveport, Louisiana.

"How'd you boys like to do a little job for me?," the voice on the phone said.

"Who is this?"

"You can call me Franklin Roosevelt.".

21

THE LIFE OF A PROFESSIONAL ATHLETE is a lot tougher than it looks. The adulation, the crowds, the sponsor obligations, appearances at children's hospitals, shooting commercials for ESPN SportsCenter while still finding time to dominate your sport.

Long Jim Steele was a professional athlete.

He had none of those problems.

"So what do you do?," the attractive woman Jim was working at the hotel bar asked.

"I'm a professional athlete."

"Really?," she was intrigued and slid a little closer. "What sport?"

"I'm a golfer."

Okay, she was a little less intrigued, but, hey, golfers make lots of money. And they go to Hawaii a lot.

"A golfer, like on TV, right?," she said. If there's one thing every American values above all else, it's that you have been or could possibly appear on TV. People will do anything to be on TV. A game show where you have to eat a pickled pig's anus and wash it down with a glass of horse sweat? If it's on TV, you'll have people lined up and wanting to know if they'll be on camera longer if they're willing to eat two pig anuses.

If you called a casting agent and asked them to send over a professional golfer, they'd send Jim Steele. He was an athletic six-foot-four, stylish haircut, winning smile, firm handshake and a polo shirt with an Odyssey Golf logo on it. This guy screamed professional golfer.

"So you've been on TV?"

"Sure, plenty of times." She was thinking ESPN and CBS while he was thinking Good Morning Terre Haute.

"Where do you play?," she asked.

"All over. Indiana, Ohio, New Jersey."

"Um, California?"

"Oh sure, California, all the time." If that's what needed to happen for Jim Steele to close the deal with this woman, then that's what was going to happen. Jim's idea of a long-term relationship was 72 hours. Not long ago he'd been with a woman, Darla or Darlene or something like that, for almost 80 hours. He found the whole thing suffocating.

"Being a pro golfer must be so cool, are you on the tour?"

Uh-oh, she knows about golf. Jim told himself to stay cool, he'd been in this spot before.

"Oh sure, been on the tour for years."

"The PGA Tour?"

"No, the PPUS."

"Is that like the Nationwide Tour?"

Wow, big golf fan. This isn't going to go well, he thought.

"Kind of."

"PPUS. What does that stand for?"

"Professional Putters of the United States."

"Pus?"

"We don't call it that."

"Putting as in putt-putt? You're a professional putt-putt player?," she said smiling.

"Putting is the most challenging part of the game. Like they say, drive for show, putt for dough."

"A lot of money in the professional putting game?"

"I do okay."

"Oh really?"

"The keys to a brand new Honda Civic didn't jump into my pocket all by themselves."

Jim was cool under fire. That's how you win the coveted Gold Cup, sponsored by Gold Bond Powder (America's leading athlete's foot and jock itch powder, try the new cooling menthol flavor), which is the biggest prize in the putting world.

Jim had two Gold Cups, one more and he would receive the Platinum Putter, the grand slam of the putting world.

"So what do you find the most difficult kind of hole, the windmill or the big clown face? Myself, I find the clown face kind of creepy, but I block it out. The windmill stumps me every time."

Three strikes and Jim was out.

Fortunately, someone had just texted him.

It read "Help."

Leonard's phone started to ring.

Jimmy pointed the vintage revolver at Leonard and said, "Nice and easy, act like nothing's wrong. Be cool. Okay, answer it."

"Hello," Leonard said.

"I'm guessing you're in some kind of trouble," Jim said.

"Why would you say that?"

"Because you texted the word 'help' to my phone. I'm pretty quick."

"Right, right, I could see how you'd think that. I ran out of gas."

"That's why you texted the word 'help?'"

"Not entirely."

"Okay, I'm calling your Uncle Arnie."

"What? No! He's a 75-year-old man who can't even remember which war he fought in. Have you lost your mind?"

"I'm calling him because," Jim said, "you installed the Where's My Phone app on his computer. If I go to his house I can figure out where you are and try to help your dumb bowler ass."

"For a guy who can't hit a golf ball more than ten yards, you're pretty smart."

"Don't do anything stupid. Or anything more stupid than you've already done."

Bowlers don't usually have groupies, but Leonard had the biggest fan any athlete could ever have. His mother's oldest brother, Arnie Rubenstein.

Not exactly the kind of groupie you'd expect to find on Bret Michaels' tour bus, but if you needed somebody to have your back, Uncle Arnie was the man you wanted. He was wiry, he was tough, he was resourceful and giving up wasn't in his vocabulary.

Just ask the International Olympic Committee.

Arnie believed in America, believed in the power of good over evil and, more than anything else, he believed in Leonard Fleischman. He appointed himself Leonard's manager and took it as his personal mission to get bowling into the Olympics.

"Uncle Arnie," Leonard said, "I appreciate you trying to get bowling into the Olympics and everything, but what's the rush?"

"You're young, you think you're indestructible, that you're going to be at the peak of your athletic powers forever. But trust me, Leonard, one day you'll step up to that line and you won't be as strong as you used to be and your back will hurt and you'll have to go to the bathroom every 15 goddamn minutes and you'll have all kinds of hair growing out of your ears and you can't remember shit and you'll think, well, at least I was in the Olympics."

"Thanks for the pep talk, Uncle Arnie."

"You might even win a medal. At least a bronze."

"You really know how to build a guy up."

"Let me ask you a question, Lenny."

"Shoot."

"Did you know that the International Olympic Committee is headquartered in a foreign country?"

"Yes."

"And not just any foreign country, but Switzerland."

"I knew that, Uncle Arnie."

"Switzerland is what's called a neutral country. You know what that means? They didn't take sides in World War II. They just stood by and let the Nazis take over the United Nations."

"I'm not sure that's how it happened."

"I can tell you this much, Leonard, I didn't fight in the Battle of the Bulge to let some we-don't-want-to-take-sides country run our Olympic games."

"I thought you fought in Korea?"

"While Mussolini and the Greeks were making the trains run on time I was waist deep in a Vietnamese swamp."

Uncle Arnie was either an infantryman in World War II, a helicopter mechanic in Korea or a sniper in Vietnam. Maybe two of the above, but probably not all three. As the years went by the stories grew more jumbled and way more exciting. Wrestled shirtless with Dwight Eisenhower, named the Korean Demilitarized Zone ("it just came to me," Uncle Arnie said) and explained to a young private named Joseph Heller about the Army concept known as Catch-22. Leonard had thought about checking with the Army or the Navy or the Marines to check his service record, but he figured the truth would never hold a candle to the stories.

Although one of his stories had at least a little bit of truth to it.

"I took this gun off of Joseph Goebbels' assistant's cousin," Uncle Arnie said. "I want you to have it."

"Is it real?"

"Of course it's real, look at this," he snapped open the magazine of the old Luger to show him that it was loaded to the hilt. "Locked and loaded with the Third Reich's best. Take it, you never know. Bowling is safe, but the Olympics, now that's dangerous business."

Leonard was no hero, but if he had to, he could make a play for the Luger sitting in the glovebox.

He knew help was on the way.

He just didn't know how much.

22

"IF WE WERE IN MISSISSIPPI someone would have stopped by now," Jimmy said.

"What'd he say?," Bernie said.

"He said, if we were in Mississippi someone would have stopped by now," Timmy translated.

"Why, to rob us?," Leonard said.

"Jackson, Mississippi is a very safe place. As long as you stay where you're supposed to stay and don't shoot your mouth off and you keep a little gun in your pocket."

"Sounds great."

Then help arrived. And arrived. And arrived.

A black Suburban pulled up behind them and switched on the flashers. Then a Cadillac sedan slid to a stop in front of them. The door opened wide and slammed hard into the guard rail. A very muscular man with an eyepatch, an arm sling and an orthopedic boot struggled out. He kicked the door closed with the boot and started to huff over to Leonard's car. Then a Chevy Cavalier stopped, but not just any Cavalier, a car that had scorch marks around all the windows and a melted interior that looked like a Salvador Dali painting. The steering wheel was shaped like a lower case g. A man with no eyebrows and all the hair burned off the left side of his head climbed out. He had an eyepatch, too. The doors to the Suburban swung open ceremoniously to allow a large, athletic man to step out of the driver's seat and a small, hard looking woman out on the passenger side. Both were wearing matching black suits. Neither were wearing eye patches.

The collection of tough guys and gals walked, strolled and hobbled to form a gauntlet around the dead Dodge Neon.

Leonard rolled down the window.

"Car trouble?," Big Mike said, actually stringing together two words.

"Out of gas, wait a minute," Leonard says, "is that you, Sally? The Crock Pot guy?"

"Oh yeah, hey Leonard."

"What happened to you? Are you alright?"

"I was burning a candle in my apartment and it got out of control."

"You were burning a candle in your apartment?," Big Mike asked. "Was it lavender scented to go with your panties?"

"Fuck you, Mike."

"Make me."

"Is anyone actually going to help us?," asked Jimmy, but no one could understand him.

"What happened to your car?," Leonard said. "The whole interior is melted."

"Candle."

"You were burning a candle in your car?," Leonard started to get out and take a look.

The big guy in the black suit came over and shoved the door closed.

"Why don't you just stay in the car, sir," Mr. 176

said.

"Who the hell are you?," said Jimmy and jumped out of the car just to make a point. Since he had two black eyes and a broken arm, it wasn't much of a point. "It's a free country and I can do whatever the hell I want."

"Gun!," the woman in the black suit shouted when she spotted the rusty revolver stuffed into Jimmy's waistband.

Suddenly, everyone had a gun. Big Mike pulled a Glock out of from under his track suit jacket, nearly dropping it because he was doing everything left-handed. Ms. 191 produced her Wisco-issued H&K .40 and Mr. 176 shouldered an old school MAC-10 machine pistol.

The Crock Pot automatically put his hands up.

"Everybody take it easy," Ms. 191 said. "This doesn't have to get ugly." She looked around at Big Mike, Jimmy, Timmy and the Crock Pot. "Well, any uglier than it already is."

"I said it was a candle accident," Crock Pot said.

"We just want the old man and the ball. We'll grab them and be on our way."

"Did she say old man?," Bernie said to no one in particular.

"What's in it for us?," Jimmy said.

"What did he say?," 191 said.

"What's in it for us?," Timmy said. "We kidnapped the guy and we're not doing it for free."

"So you're admitting to kidnapping which just happens to be a federal offense."

"Are you guys Feds?"

"We're bigger than that."

"Here's the deal, you can have this guy if we get

ten grand in cash."

"That's all I'm worth? Ten grand?"

"We don't normally negotiate with kidnappers, but I will make you one counteroffer. You give us Bernie Steers and his magic bowling ball and we won't kill you right here."

The Crock Pot was taking mental notes. He didn't know who this woman was, but she really knew how to shake someone down.

While Jimmy and Timmy thought about her offer, Big Mike took a chance.

"I just want Leonard. I'll grab him and get out of your hair."

"Hold on, sir. I can't let you do that."

"Listen, lady, you need to mind your own fucking business."

"I'm not sure who that man is, but he is wearing a shirt that is issued only to professionals who are part of the Wisco Pro Bowling team. We are duty bound to protect those members at all costs."

"You have got to be shitting me," Big Mike said.

"Now you listen to me," Jimmy said trying to take control, "this here's the revolver my great, great grandpappy carried at Gettysburg."

"I thought it was Appomattox," Timmy corrected.

"What? No, mama always said it was Gettysburg," Jimmy said.

"Appomattox!"

"Whatever. My grandpappy carried this pistol either at Appomattox or Gettysburg and we're not the kind of family that backs down from a fight."

"And do you know what happened to ol' grandpappy at either Appomattox or Gettysburg?," 191 asked.

"Killed. Friendly fire, I think."

"Shocking."

If four cars weren't enough, another one rolled up to the scene bringing with it what appeared to be a professional golfer holding a gold painted putter in a threatening manner. As much as a putter can be held in a threatening manner.

"Okay people," Jim Steele said, "let's all, whoa, everybody has guns."

"I don't," said Crock Pot.

"Leonard, are you okay?"

"Not really."

"Wait a minute, buddy, I'm here now and we're going to get you out of here."

The passenger door of the car opened and a frail, old man in some sort of hodgepodge military uniform made up of a pair of Marine uniform trousers, an olive drab Vietnam-era shirt with the name "Rubenstein" over the pocket and a World War I doughboy helmet. And a samurai sword.

"Just a goddamn minute here. I didn't fight the Nazis at Inchon just to have some Communists come over here and try to kill my Leonard," the old soldier of undetermined rank or service said.

"I'm not a Communist," Big Mike protested.

"I'm not a Communist, either," Timmy said, "we're Methodist."

"Enough," 191 said. "We're taking Steers and the ball and we're going." She started moving toward the car.

"Hold on there, little lady, nobody's doing anything until my brother and I get our ten thousand dollars. I'll kill him before I'll let you have him." Jimmy leveled the old revolver at Bernie's head and pulled back the hammer.

Screech. Click.

Jimmy and Timmy's first kidnapping was not going to end well, but they were going to make sure it ended on their terms.

191 started moving fast toward Jimmy.

Jimmy pulled the trigger.

They say events like shootings seem to happen in slow motion. This one certainly did. Jimmy yanked on the trigger and the hammer fell. Next came a sort of sizzling sound, a gentle puff of blue smoke and, finally, an audible sigh oozed from the gun. Jimmy gave it a shake and a generous amount of rust poured out of the barrel.

"Maybe it got wet at Gettysburg," Jimmy said.

"Appomattox," Timmy said.

"What?"

But Jimmy never really got the word "What" all the way out, because 191 had closed on him, slapped her left hand against his ear and then drove the heel of her right hand into Jimmy's bandaged nose smashing it flat against the rest of his face. For good measure, she introduced her knee to his testicles.

As Jimmy was going down, Big Mike saw an opportunity to make his move. Unfortunately, it was a bad one. 191 sensed him starting to move, so she wheeled on him next. A sidekick into his shin snapped his tibia and fibula and gravity took over from there. Just to make sure she had made her point, she chopped him in the throat on his way down.

She stepped back to survey any additional threats.

"I'm good," said Crock Pot.

"Me, too," said Timmy.

Bernie couldn't believe what he was seeing.

"Step out of the car, Mr. Steers," 191 said.

"I always thought this was a legend, a myth of some kind," Bernie said, mouth hanging open. "I can't believe you guys are real."

"We are very much real, sir."

"Bernie, who are these people?," Leonard asked.

"They're members of the elite Wisco Security Team. I thought they were just ghosts or made up to scare the guys over at Pinknockerz, they're a crack security team charged with protecting Wisco Corporation's bowling secrets and, by extension, preserving the game of bowling. They have a license to kill."

"That part is just a rumor," said 176, "but that would be super cool."

"I can't confirm or deny any of that, sir," 191 said, "but I need to see your balls."

"Bet that's the first time any woman's ever asked you that," Timmy said.

191 turned toward Timmy. He flinched and shut up.

176 grabbed the public television tote bag.

"You disguised the world's first self-correcting bowling ball as a Pinknockerz Pincracker?," 191 said. "That's either brilliant or insane."

"Um," Bernie said, "that's not my bag. Or my ball. My daughter must have grabbed the wrong bag."

"Daughter. Susie. Aged 23. Named after Earl Anthony's wife," 176 dutifully reported. "Been in and out of college and junior college for the last five years. No degree. No job. No priors."

"Where'd she go?," 191 asked.

"I don't know," Bernie answered.

The two Wisco agents jumped back into their

Suburban and sped away. Mike and Jimmy were still moaning on the ground. Timmy was trying to patch up his brother as best he could.

"I'm still out of gas," Leonard said.

"I may have some in my car," Crock Pot said.

23

SURGEONS ARE KNOWN for going to great lengths to protect their hands. Bowlers, not so much.

Which is how Joe Gleer, winner of the Centereach regional bowling qualifier, explained his poorly timed injury to the reporter from the Centereach Daily Mirror-Intelligencer.

"I'm just a klutz, I guess," Gleer explained to the reporter, "kind of bad timing, too."

Just two days before the highly anticipated Jani-San Custodial Services 100 Grand Bowling Invitational, presented by Scratch-Eze Antifungal Spray, was scheduled to be held at the world-famous Meadowlands in scenic East Rutherford, New Jersey, Mr. Gleer broke his right hand, his bowling hand, in spectacular fashion.

"I tripped over the cat and fell off the porch. Caught myself right on my bowling hand. Busted it up pretty good." He sounded sad, but resolved to deal with his bad luck. "It's a tough break, but at least I'm alive, right?"

That was the public story. The cops weren't buying it.

The police report showed Mr. Greer suffered several broken fingers, cracked metatarsals, a shattered wrist, dislocated elbow and a separated shoulder. He was also sporting a swollen, puffy, broken nose. Injuries that would put even a professional athlete out of commission for 10 to 12 weeks. The injuries, according to the ER doc who treated him, seemed a lot more consistent with being beaten with a claw hammer than tripping over a cat and falling off a porch. Right down to the telltale crosshatch pattern in his lacerations that matched up perfectly to the face of the claw hammer found in the victim's garage. The claw hammer that had just been washed.

"Why did you wash your hammer?," the police asked Joe.

"Because it was dirty."

"Who washes a hammer? I've had the same hammer for 20 years and I've never washed it. Never even thought about washing it."

"I'm a man who likes a clean hammer. Any crime in that?"

The real story was summed up in two words: Ray. Flanagan.

Ray stopped by Joe Gleer's house and asked him nicely if he'd like to give up his spot in the Meadowlands tournament. Ray explained about his liver and his wife and his shot off ear. When Joe declined, Ray asked him if he'd like a nice ass kicking instead. Apparently, that was the option Joe chose. Ray grabbed him by the arm, twisted the shoulder out of the socket and dragged him into the garage where he beat his right hand into mush with his own hammer.

Joe Gleer's unfortunate injury forced him to give his position to the first alternate.

Ray was in. Now he had to make sure he was going to win.

"Where is my magic fucking bowling ball?," said Mr. 221. He wasn't in a very good mood.

"The daughter has it," Jimmy said.

"And where is the daughter?"

"We're getting back to work on that as soon as we get out of here."

"Let me guess, you paid another visit to the emergency room?"

"Just a quick one. We ran into a little trouble while we were with your Bernie Steers guy."

"When you 'were' with him? Is that to imply you aren't with him anymore?"

"He didn't have the ball anyway."

"Why aren't you idiots with him anymore?"

"Like I said, we ran into a little trouble."

"Let me guess. The trouble was about five-foot-two, black suit, throws a mean straight right to the nose?"

"Yeah, how'd you know?"

"She works for me."

"What? Well, you tell her I'm gonna kick her ass next time I see her."

"Good luck."

"She's on my fucking radar."

"And I'll put you on her radar if I don't get that ball."

"What's the big damn deal about this ball?"

"It's going to change the world. It's the bowling equivalent of the One Ring from Lord of the Rings,

Harry Potter's wand and a pair of ruby red slippers jammed inside the Ark of the Covenant. Not something that should be unleashed on the world at a New Jersey beerfest."

"Whatever. How about a raise?"

"How about you do what you're told or they'll never find a part of your body bigger than a dime."

"Gotcha loud and clear, boss."

"What'd he say?," Timmy said.

"We're still on the job. And he's still an asshole."

"Hello?"

"If you're trying to stay undercover, you should probably stop answering your phone."

"Hello, Susie."

"Hi Dad. Have you called mom yet?"

"No, it's better that she, uh...listen, where are you? Wait a minute, don't tell me, they might be listening."

"Who, the NSA?"

"No, the Wisco Security Team."

"Who?"

"It's a super secret security detail from Wisco corporate. I thought it was just a rumor, but they really exist."

"Oh I'm so scared. What are they going to do when they find me, tie the laces of my bowling shoes together?"

"I just saw one of them knock that country bumpkin out cold with one shot then spin around and break some other big guy's leg. Rumor is they have rocket-propelled grenades. They're very dangerous people. And they're trying to find you,

Susie."

"What do they want?"

"My bowling ball."

"This piece of crap?"

"That piece of crap is a computer-controlled, micro hydraulic-activated, self-correcting, experimental bowling ball system with about eight hundred thousand dollars worth of technology crammed into it. Go ahead, bowl with it."

"I'll have to, since you have my ball."

"Speaking of that, what in God's name are you doing with a Pinknockerz bowling ball?"

"Ethan got it for me."

"You mean that boy with all the piercings in his face?"

"Yes."

"And the purple hair?"

"Yes."

"And the words 'fuck' and 'you' tattooed on his knuckles?"

"Yes," she sighed.

"Your mother didn't like him very much."

"That's the problem."

"Your mother?"

"No. You. You were either working on bowling balls or watching bowling or thinking about bowling. And whenever we talked, you never really talked to me. Ethan had nothing to do with mom, but you push it off on her to keep from expressing your feelings."

"Listen, Susie, I'm not a big feelings kind of guy. I'm an engineer, it's not a real touchy feely occupation."

"But I was a kid. I needed my daddy. Ethan was

me acting out, trying to get your attention."

"You sound like some kind of shrink."

"Dad, I was in therapy for the last five years."

Bernie was staggered.

"I'm, I'm sorry, I didn't know. I'm so sorry."

"It's okay."

"No it's not. I didn't see it. I was wrong. But look, I'm here, you're here. We have the opportunity to change the bowling world. We can do it together. Will you give me a chance?"

"To do what?"

"To be your daddy."

"I'd like that."

"But the Pinknockerz ball, that really hurts."

"I used it just to piss you off," she laughed a little through some tears.

"Mission accomplished."

"It's a nice ball, Dad. Go ahead, bowl with it. Be a little open minded. We'll meet up later at an undisclosed location."

"A local bowling alley?"

"You're like a mind reader."

Susie was sitting on a barstool at Massapequa Pin and Pub drinking a diet Coke and eating a hot dog. A man in a cheap tan suit slid over to the stool next to her.

"I've never seen you in here before," Hanrahan said.

"Go fuck yourself, Grandpa."

"I'm a policeman, I could arrest you for that kind of language."

"I will knock your balls into your throat, you creepy bastard."

"If that's what you're into."

Susie grabbed her bag and moved over to a lane.

"You are one smooth talker, Hanrahan," Al offered. "Does that line usually work?"

"Nope. Never."

"But you're sticking with it. You may be stupid, but you're persistent."

"I could arrest you for calling me stupid."

"But you won't. You'd have to get off that barstool and do some police work."

"In that case, I'll have another gin and tonic."

Susie pulled the dull, blue ball out of the bag. No logo, no fancy name like Thor or Pin Pounder 6000. Just a plain ball with some weird numbers and three holes drilled in it. Let's see what the old man's been working on all these years.

She did her normal warm up routine, focused more on footwork than the pins. If six or eight went down, that was fine, she'd focus on the pins after a few throws.

First roll, the ball hooks into the pocket and nine go down. Dumb luck. Happens to 8-year-olds at birthday parties every weekend.

On the second roll she throws it a little harder, the ball hooks up at exactly the right spot, turns hard and smashes through the pocket, strike.

Two more balls, two more strikes.

Then a nine-spare. Then two more strikes. And an eight-spare.

What the hell was this thing, she thought. Time to get serious.

Susie hunkered down and rolled a 260 and then a 265. Her previous lifetime high was a 220 and that was a few years ago when she was really working on her game. This wasn't a bowling ball, it was a pin-seeking drone. This would make a 300 game no big deal. Everyone would be bowling like a pro after three or four shots. This could make bowling the most popular sport in the world.

For two weeks.

Then it would be ruined forever, cast on the obsolete game pile with Connect Four and Mystery Date.

"I've got something here," a Wisco security tech told Mr. 221.

"What's up?"

"Just something weird, really weird. It's the signature of the Bernie Steers' ball, but it's not him."

Mr. 221 squinted over the tech's shoulder at the screen.

"That's definitely not Bernie."

A shrill tone came out of the computer.

"But that's definitely a 300."

24

THE SUBURBAN SLAMMED on its brakes and skidded to a stop under the carport at Massapequa Pin and Pub sending a gaggle of eight- and nine-year-olds in all directions and causing some poor mom to drop two hundred thousand Legos all over the ground. The doors to the Suburban swung open and two figures in black suits jumped out.

"I'll cover the back, you go in the front," 191 said. "Let's get her and the ball and get out. No trouble, nice and easy."

The electric sliding front doors whooshed open for Mr. 176 who stepped through and scanned the inside of the building. There, on Lane 18, was the woman that matched the picture the home office sent to his smartphone. The trick would be to get close without spooking her toward the other exit. 176 kept moving slowly, casually. As casually as a man wearing a black suit and sunglasses inside a bowling alley during the middle of the day could. He slid past the front counter and Al didn't even look up. Of course, Al wouldn't have looked up if Sasquatch had walked in. No one really noticed Mr. 176.

Except Big Mike.

"Hey!," yelled Big Mike. "You're that guy. The guy

in the suit."

Not expecting to find a target of his revenge right under his nose, Big Mike didn't have a plan, so he went with the old stand by. Start shooting. Across a bowling alley. With a handgun. Left-handed. While wearing an eye patch and sitting in a motorized scooter with both his legs in casts. Mike started to send rounds downrange. The pro shop window shattered, the front door glass cracked and bowlers hit the floor while dialing 911.

Mr. 176 may not have been the world's best bowler, but he was expertly trained in a wide variety of tactical weapons. He was a decorated marksman with handguns, rifles, mortars, rocket propelled grenades and the MAC-10 machine gun he now had up to his shoulder. Consistent with his training, he acquired a good sight picture and sent three quick rounds 150 feet across the alley and landed two in Big Mike's shoulder.

Nice grouping, Mike thought, as he crumpled to the carpet.

After neutralizing the threat, 176 planned to acquire his next target, grab her and head back to the extraction point in the carport.

The last thing he saw was the bowling ball.

It all happened so fast, the birthday party mom was still out in the driveway trying to scoop up gazillions of scattered Lego bricks. The woman in the black suit jumped back into the Suburban, dropped it into drive and stomped on the gas. Birthday party mom dove out of the way just in time to be pelted by a rapid fire barrage of Lego bricks flying out from under the truck's spinning rear tires.

In less than two minutes the place was surrounded

by the Nassau County police. Finally, they had an excuse to fire up their brand new MRAP Armored Personnel Carrier with the high-pressure water cannon on the roof. (Thanks taxpayers!) The doors flung open and eight fully equipped riot police, complete with AR-15 assault rifles, poured out and took up positions under the carport.

"Ow, this is killing my knees," one officer said.

"What the hell is this crap?," another asked.

"It looks like a million crushed Lego pieces."

"Some kind of trap to slow us down?"

"Step on one of these when you get up in the middle of the night to take a leak and it'll slow you down plenty."

Unfortunately, the police had nothing to do except stare at a big, unconscious guy in a black suit. At least they got to walk around and look menacing which counts for something.

After the ambulance took Big Mike to the emergency room to get another hole in his frequent visitor punch card, the cops had questions. Starting with the cop on the scene.

"This is the second time this place got shot to hell with you sitting in the bar, Hanrahan," the detective said.

"Just lucky, I guess."

"What'd you see?"

"The jarhead in the black suit comes walking in here like he's looking for something. Scanning all the lanes so hard, I can hear the rusty gears turning in his stupid head. The big guy with the casts on both his legs comes out of the office in the back, pulls out a gun and starts unloading all over the place. Then, black suit man whips out a machine gun and puts two in the big guy's shoulder. Hell of a shot from all the way over there. I'm guessing he's former military. Then this chick comes out of nowhere, cold cocks the jarhead with a bowling ball and takes off. That's about it."

"And what were you doing when all this was going down?"

"I'm no idiot, I took cover when the shooting started."

"Did you draw your weapon?"

"By the time I did it was all over."

The detective looked up from his notebook and stopped writing. He closed the book and slipped it back into his jacket pocket.

"Here's the problem, Hanrahan. The guy in the black suit didn't have a machine gun. He didn't have a weapon at all. Not even one of those little pocket knives with the toothpick in it. Which means what you're telling me isn't true. What I have to figure out is why you're lying. Either you're covering something up, you're blind, stupid or just so hammered you didn't see what happened at all."

"Bullshit, I know exactly what I saw. He fired three times. Two went into the guy and one went into the wall. Check it yourself."

"Check it myself? There are 350 bullet holes in the walls left over from the last time you let the place get shot up. Listen, Hanrahan, I know you can see the pension checks from here, but you're still a cop and you'd better crawl your ass out of that whiskey bottle you're living in."

Hanrahan was pissed. He didn't know who that guy in the black suit was, but anyone who could be standing between him and his pension was an enemy that had to be dealt with now. Hanrahan was going to find this guy and get him out of the picture. And who was the woman who clonked the big guy with the bowling ball? With his cushy retirement on the line, Tommy Hanrahan was going to have to do the one thing he hated more than anything: detective work.

When Mr. 176 came to he found himself in the interview room at the Nassau County police headquarters. The entire left side of his face was red, blue, green and yellow, but mostly swollen. Had they bothered to look closely, like they do on TV crime lab shows, they would have seen the very slight indentation of the letters "BX 300.9" in reverse on his cheek.

"Look who's awake," said the detective who had watched a few too many of those shows on TV.

The Wisco Security Team all underwent extensive anti-interrogation training in case they fell into the wrong hands. Mr. 176 was more than a match for some local cop.

"Why don't you tell me what happened."

"Wisco Bowling Special Agent Brandon Krause, 23301," said Mr. 176, sticking to his training.

"What?," the detective asked.

"Wisco Bowling Special Agent Brandon Krause, 23301."

"Name, rank and serial number?"

"Name, rank and PBA number."

"PBA number?"

"Professional Bowlers Association membership number."

"Are you shitting me?"

After a long pause, Mr. 176 said, "Am I under arrest?"

"You're not under arrest, but I have some questions for you. Starting with, what the hell happened in that bowling alley?"

"I don't recall."

"Why did someone knock you out with a bowling ball?"

"Random crime I suppose, New York is a very dangerous place."

"What are you doing in New York?"

"I'm traveling on business."

"What kind of business?"

"Bowling business. Confidential bowling business."

"Do you want to file charges against the person who hit you?"

"No, I do not. Am I free to go or are you going to bring out the rubber hose?"

The detective sighed.

"We didn't find a gun on you and, even in the State of New York, it is not a crime to be stupid enough to get hit in the head with a bowling ball."

"Am I free to go?"

"You are free to go."

"One question for you."

"Yes?"

"What's the best way to get to the Meadowlands?"

"Why do you want to go to the Meadowlands?"

"Wisco Bowling Special Agent Brandon Krause, 23301."

"Get the hell out of my police station."

"Hello?"

"Dad, it's Susie."

"Are you alright?"

"I think so, but they're everywhere, they're trying to get me."

"I'm coming to get you, baby."

"Hurry. And Dad."

"Yeah."

"That is one hell of a bowling ball."

"I know, right?"

25

THE WAYFARER DINER on Nesconset Highway was a pretty typical Long Island diner. Done in the style of shiny 1950's chrome diners meant to evoke the glamorous bygone days of railroad dining cars. Fortunately, no one is left who accurately remembers how horrible the food was in railroad dining cars, so the fantasy still has some life in it.

People who frequent these diners liked to think of them as a crossroads of America. A place where people from all walks of life gather to eat a good-tasting meal served by a big-hearted waitress and exchange the local news of the day. In many ways, these diners were the very heartbeats of the communities they served.

All of which was total bullshit.

The Long Island diner concept peaked in 1971 and has streaked downhill ever since. Marked by poorly prepared, outdated food, cranky waitresses doing a job they hate for reasons they hate even more, owners who could not care less that you're even there and 24 hour operation that owes its existence to some less-than-thorough health department inspections.

The menus are pretty similar from diner to diner.

Monday special: Pot roast with carrots and peas

Tuesday special: Beef stew (basically, the leftover pot roast, carrots and peas)

Wednesday special: Fried scrod (too horrible to even think about)

Thursday special: Mom's Meat Loaf (Using "Mom's Special Recipe," which is basically the cheapest possible ground beef a few days passed the "sell by" date, bound together with stale rolls recycled from the tables of customers who left them behind)

Friday special: Gyros and Greek Salad (Every Long Island diner must, by law, serve this)

The real reason Long Island's diners have thrived for all these years is simple. Full bar day and night.

Want your meat loaf with a shot of Jameson's and a draft beer? No problem.

A three-egg ham and cheese omelet with a Manhattan? Coming right up.

They can even recommend a few cocktails that will leave your breath fresh and minty instead of creepy and boozy.

The Wayfarer was in a great location. It did a wonderful business with the local alcoholics as well as the commuting drunks who needed a quick pop or two on the way to and from their jobs in New York City. It was owned by a Lebanese immigrant named Samir who hated talking to the customers more than life itself and was managed by his son "Johnnie" who ran a thriving side business selling weed out the back door.

In the last booth by the windows sat Bernie, Susie and Leonard, their bowling bags on the ground next to their feet. The waitress threw down three greasy menus and sweaty juice glasses filled with lukewarm water.

"Get you something to drink?," half assed the waitress.

"Just water," said Leonard.

"Water with lemon," said Susie.

"Pepsi," said Bernie.

"Who actually orders Pepsi on purpose?," Leonard said.

"I like it," Bernie said, "I am part of the Pepsi generation."

The waitress sighed and wandered off. If they weren't drinking, they weren't tipping.

"What happened at the bowling alley?," Leonard asked. "It's all over the news."

"I'm in there throwing a few games with the magic ball and I hear some big steroided up dude yelling from the back of the bowling alley."

"Crew cut, no neck, both feet in casts?"

"That's him."

"Big Mike."

"We met him on the side of the road. Charming guy," Bernie said.

"So Big Mike starts yelling at this other big guy in a black suit who just walked in. Black Suit Guy is looking straight at me and starts walking my way when Big Mike pulls a pistol out of his pants and lets it rip. And this guy can't hit shit. Bullets are flying all over the place, glass is breaking, people are screaming."

"It's not the first time," Leonard said.

"Then it gets really crazy. The guy in the black suit whips out some kind of tiny machine gun. He takes aim and drops Big Mike with a couple of shots. It was freaking awesome. I'm not interested in sticking around to see how this works out, so I'm heading for the door. I'm almost past Mr. Men In Black, when he turns and sees me. So I clonk him on the side of the head with the bowling ball and he goes down, too. Then I hit the door just in time to see this tiny woman in a matching black suit grab the big guy's machine gun, jump into a creepy black Suburban and peel out of there."

"Okay, let's figure out where we are," Bernie said.

"You mean, who is trying to kill us?," Susie said.

"We can't be emotional, we have to approach this from a logical, engineering point of view."

The waitress reappeared looking more bedraggled than before, if that was even possible.

"Ready to order?," she asked.

"Can we have a few more minutes?," Leonard said.

"Sure, hon," sighed the waitress.

"Okay, quick list of everyone who wants to kill us," said Susie.

They took out a napkin to write on, but no one had a pen.

"Excuse me," Leonard asked the waitress, "can we borrow your pen?"

"Sure," she said, "ready to order anything?"

"Do you have cappuccino?," Susie asked.

"It's a diner, dear, not a Starbucks."

"Nothing for me, thanks."

Pen in hand, they got back to the napkin and made a list of everyone who wanted them dead and what their current status was.

Jimmy and Timmy Duval. Status unknown, probably in the hospital.

The Wisco Security Team. The big guy, status unknown, probably in the hospital or in jail.

The woman, on the loose. Super dangerous,

heavily armed, license to kill (internet rumor).

Big Mike. Both feet in orthopedic boot casts, one arm in a sling, two bullets in the shoulder. Eyepatch. Should be in the hospital, probably isn't. Injured, armed, dangerous, crazy.

Crock Pot. Whereabouts unknown. Status unknown. Could be dangerous, could be a doofus.

The list wasn't looking good.

"Oh yeah," Leonard said. "One more. There's this bowler named Ray who is severely pissed at me for beating him. He's big, he's strong and he coughs up blood all the time."

"Is that supposed to be his super power?," Susie asked.

"It's pretty gross," Leonard answered. "But he's a hell of a bowler."

"So here's what we know," Bernie summed up. "We have at least seven people who would like to see at least one of us dead."

"Maybe we should just go to the police," Leonard said.

"That would be good. We can tell them some mafia hit men, Hee-Haw castoffs and elite members of a bowling ball company security team want to kill us so they can steal our magic bowling ball and prevent us from winning a tournament co-sponsored by a janitorial services company and a manufacturer of anti fungal shoe spray," Susie said. "I'm thinking they'll scramble the fighter jets as soon as they hear that one."

"That about sums it up," Leonard said.

"They'll put us all in straight jackets," Bernie said. "Maybe we can reason with the killers. You know, just sit down and talk like adults."

"Where should we start, Dad? With the robots from Wisco, the hit men from Long Island or the blood vomiting superhero? Listen guys, can't we all just talk this out?"

"Your sarcasm isn't helping, young lady," Bernie said.

They all just stared at the blank spaces where their beef stew would have been had the waitress ever returned to take their orders.

"It's always been my dream to be a professional bowler," said Leonard. "This was going to be my big chance. I don't even care about the money, I just wanted to go on the PBA tour and prove myself."

"Leonard, you need to win that tournament," Bernie said brightening with an idea. "Use the BX300.9, you'll kill everybody."

"I can't do it. I don't want to win that way. I think I'm good enough to have a chance to win outright."

"Then let's go," Susie said. "Let's get you to the tournament, keep all seven of these people from killing you and we'll make bowling history."

"She's got a point," Bernie said. "The tournament is going to be televised on live TV, well cable anyway, and nobody is going to try to kill you on live television. That tournament is probably the safest, most secure place in the world right now."

"Where is this stupid tournament anyway?"

"It's at the Meadowlands."

"The Meadowlands," Susie said. "That sounds nice."

"In New Jersey."

"Oh."

26

THE MEADOWLANDS ON A SUNDAY during football season was considered one of the safest, most secure places in the nation. Tight security, metal detectors, strict rules regarding what can and cannot be brought into the stadium. The highly trained security team that executes this program week in and week out prides itself on being one of the very best in the business.

Too bad none of them were at the Meadowlands today.

The promoters of the Jani-San 100 Grand Invitational Tournament, presented by Scratch-Eze Antifungal Spray, were not putting on this event for their love of bowling. They were in it for the money and that meant maximizing profits wherever possible. The rental for the Meadowlands was a little higher than they thought, plus the taxes, the insurance and everything else, so they cut a few corners to make things work.

Since this was a bowling tournament, they decided to make sure they had plenty of money committed to the important things like hot dogs, beer and ball caps with the Jani-San logo on them and didn't worry so much about paying for things like ambulances or security. Ever tried to rent a metal detector? Very expensive. And those ambulance drivers, who wants to pay them to sit around all day?

There would, however, be a full contingent of parking lot attendants.

"Okay team," said Ricky, today's head of security, who would normally be helping people select toilet repair parts at the local Home Depot store, "here's how it's gonna go. We're going to have four gates open. Make sure the people who are coming in have tickets. It is very important that people have tickets."

"Is that because they had to undergo a strict background check in the process of getting their tickets?," asked 23-year-old Glen Ryan, a police officer wannabe who had failed the academy admission test three times and based his vast store of police tactical knowledge on old episodes of Hill Street Blues.

"No," Ricky explained. "It's because if they don't have tickets, the boss isn't making any money and making money keeps the boss happy."

"Should we be on the lookout for anyone trying to smuggle in anything in particular?," Glen probed.

"What are you talking about? It's a bowling tournament, no one's trying to sneak in heroin or stolen kidneys or anything."

"What about beer?," an actual intelligent person offered.

"Good thinking back there, whoever you are," Ricky said. "We can't have people sneaking in beer. We need them buying beer while they're here."

"Okay," Glen said. "BOLO beer and weapons."

"Who said anything about weapons?"

"It seems like that would be a given, you know,

BOLO weapons."

"Stop saying BOLO."

"Yes, sir."

"And stop calling me sir. These people are bowlers. The worst thing they could do is fall over and die on each other. Forget about the weapons."

"Check," Glen said again. "BOLO beer, forget about the weapons. By the way, will we be issued our own weapons?"

"You're kidding, right?"

"Aren't you going to say something inspirational like, 'let's be careful out there?'"

"Get out of my sight, Glen."

"That'll work."

Unarmed, untrained and focused on the apprehension of contraband alcoholic beverages, the security team was ready for a day of championship bowling action.

Getting to the Meadowlands was no easy task. First of all, it was in New Jersey. And very few people actually go to New Jersey on purpose. They might get off at the wrong exit or fly into Newark to get a cheaper airfare, but very few people are stopping by their travel agent and asking, "how's New Jersey this time of year?"

If you have a helicopter, you have options. Other than that, you're screwed. The stadium is served by several major arteries all of which are crammed with traffic whether there is a game or not. Presumably, they're all trying to find some way to get out of New Jersey. Some parts of the country take pride in their scenery or their history, New Jerseyites love their traffic.

"I sat in a traffic jam for three days once," an old timer said. "I had to boil the seat covers and eat them."

"That's nothing," another grizzled veteran offered. "My son was born in a traffic jam, by the time we got home he was in the second grade."

"Ha!," said someone else raising the ante. "I was once on the New Jersey Turnpike in a traffic jam where everyone, including me, was killed in a fiery 1,000-car crash. I recovered."

Leonard, Susie and Bernie were stuck in a pretty typical, which means horrible, traffic jam trying to get into New Jersey.

Three miles ahead of them was the Crock Pot in his Chevy Cavalier with the Salvador Dali interior package. He left early, because he needed time to execute his plan to take care of Leonard and Big Mike and fulfill his dream of becoming Hit Man of the Month. That was a thing, right?

A mile behind was Ray Flanagan. He had left the house late because he slept through his alarm. Being up all night hacking up your major organs tended to mess up your sleep patterns. So far, Ray had used his truck to force several cars into the ditch. It was hard work, but he was making good time.

Three cars behind Susie, Bernie and Leonard was the black Suburban that had been tailing them for hours since they left the Wayfarer Diner. Behind the wheel was Mr. 176 struggling a little, because he was seeing double out of his left eye. His orbital bone was fractured, his eye was swollen half shut and the white of his eye was much more like the red of his eye. Ms.

191 was in the passenger seat committing the blueprints of the Meadowlands to memory. If she needed to navigate the stadium through the air conditioning ducts, she wanted to be ready.

Tearing down the shoulder with the lights and siren blaring was the Nassau County police department's MRAP Armored Personnel Carrier. After coughing up three hundred and fifty grand in taxpayer money, they weren't about to let that thing sit around and get dusty. Especially if one of Nassau County's favorite sons was in danger. Who that favorite son was, they weren't exactly sure, but they'd figure it out on the way. All they knew was that local hit men and what they believed to be highly trained paramilitary agents from some secret international fighting force (code named "Wisco") were converging on the Meadowlands. The MRAP would be there, too, complete with a cadre of eight riot gear equipped police officers.

"Jeez, are we there yet?," complained one cop from behind his Lexan riot shield.

"Quit leaning on me, you fat bastard, there's plenty of room over there."

"It's hot, crank up the air conditioning."

"Look, if I have to stop this armored personnel carrier so you guys can have it out on the side of the road, trust me, I will."

And just turning into the parking lot of the Meadowlands was a black Cadillac, driven by Big Mike. He grabbed his handicap placard and swung it over the rear view mirror. Having both legs in casts had its advantages.

He rolled up to the parking attendant in the safety orange vest, a local they had hired for eight bucks an hour, he was ready to park some cars and then get back to complaining about his life full time.

"Fifty bucks," the attendant said.

"That's okay," Big Mike said, "I got the handicap thing."

"Doesn't matter, fifty bucks."

"What the fuck? Handicap people park for free, right up front."

"Everybody pays fifty bucks. I don't care if you're in an iron lung."

"That's bullshit."

"That's the rules. Fifty bucks or you can take your handicapped ass back to Crutchville."

"How about I get out of this car and show you how a handicapped guy can kick your ass?"

"I'm sure the New Jersey State Police would enjoy that."

He picked up his walkie-talkie and started to press the talk button.

"Alright, here's your fifty bucks, asshole."

The New Jersey State Police were not on the other end of that walkie-talkie and the parking people weren't really keeping very close tabs on how many cars were coming in and out. That fifty bucks went straight into the guy's pocket. Combat pay, he figured.

Big Mike pulled all the way up to the front to grab the nicest handicap spot he could find. He was 20 feet from the door which was sweet. Figuring he'd have to cover a lot of ground at the Meadowlands, and not wanting to do it with two casts, he grabbed his mom's Rascal scooter and tied it into the trunk of the Caddy. He also made a few modifications. Stashed in hidden compartments on the Rascal were a .45 caliber 1911 semi-automatic handgun, an old .357 Magnum revolver he had lying around, a sawed-off shotgun and a bunch of ammo for everything including the two Glocks he had jammed in each of his leg casts. Big Mike just hoped the little electric motor was strong enough to carry it all. He was pretty confident, because he had seen those things drag some pretty big people around the grocery store.

He grunted and groaned as he got out of the car and untied the Rascal. Half lifting and half dragging, he got the Rascal out of the trunk dropping it the last two feet to the ground, knocking open one of his secret compartments and sending 25 12-gauge shotgun rounds rolling all over. Mike did what he could, but a few of the shells rolled under the Cadillac too far to reach. What the hell, he had plenty more.

Mike mounted up on the Rascal and headed in.

"Ticket, please."

"I don't need a ticket, I'm handicapped," Big Mike said.

Big Mike was not entirely clear on the powers vested in the handicap placard. It did not, as it turns out, entitle you to tons of free stuff like he thought. As Mike explained, "it's like a big 'I'm sorry' note from the rest of the world. We're sorry you're busted up, Mike, so please take a bunch of free stuff while we wait for you to get better."

"Sir, I'm sorry, but everyone needs a ticket. The placard gets you a handicapped spot in the parking lot and access to handicapped seating in the stadium, but you still must have a ticket to enter."

"This is total bullshit. I'm injured. I'm handicapped. I'm a fucking cripple, can't you see?"

"Hold on a minute," said a man with a pair of crutches and some serious looking leg braces. "Don't name call. No one says 'cripple' anymore, friend. We're not able-bodied."

"I'll be completely able-bodied once my goddamned legs heal up, so get the hell out of here before I kick your crippled ass."

The man poked Mike hard in the ribs with his crutch which Mike grabbed instinctively causing the man in the leg braces to topple over. The ticket taker called security who took both of them to the little jail they have in the basement of the Meadowlands.

"I didn't think we'd have trouble at this bowling thing," Ricky, the head of security slash Home Depot Most Punctual Employee of the Week said. "And I definitely didn't think we'd have to break up two crippled guys."

"Not able-bodied!," Big Mike and the crutch man said simultaneously.

Ricky handed the two off to Gary, who fancied himself to be like the Vincent D'onfrio character in Law & Order: Criminal Intent, walked into the interview room and surveyed the two culprits. He slammed a file folder down on the table hard startling the man who was actually handicapped.

"So who would like to tell me what's going on here? How about you?"

"Listen," Big Mike said, "this is all just a big misunderstanding, can we get out of here?"

Gary leaned down close to Mike's face and said, "No one is getting out of here until I get some answers."

The walkie-talkie came to life, "Hey Gary, where'd you put the pretzels? I'm starving down here."

"They're in the storage cabinet, over."

"The storage cabinet on the floor or the one over

the desk?"

"Over the desk! I'm busy. Over."

Gary stared down the pair.

"Did you only get the stick pretzels?," the walkie crackled. "Or did you get the tiny twist kind? I really like the tiny twist kind."

"I'll be down in a minute. Stand by. Over."

"Okay, but hurry. The only thing I've had all day is a Slim Jim and a Bud Light."

Gary composed himself and turned to Mike.

"I think you're the troublemaker here and I think it's time for you to tell me what I want to know."

"Do you want to know how to go fuck yourself? Because that's pretty much all I'm going to tell you."

"Oh, so you're one of those."

"Yes, that's exactly what I am."

Mike stood up in the Rascal, grabbed Gary's arm and broke it over the edge of the table. Then he took a handful of Gary's hair and beat Gary's empty head on the desk again and again until he was out cold and blood was coming from both his ears.

Mr. Leg Braces didn't care for that move one bit.

"You are a vile and violent man. Look what you've done to him, he could have permanent brain damage."

"Then maybe he can get his own handicap placard."

"You, sir, do not deserve to carry the handicap placard, you are an affront to the handicap movement and everything it stands for."

"I don't give a shit about the handicap movement, because I'm not handicapped."

"You make me sick."

"Maybe that's why your legs don't work."

Mike put the Rascal in reverse and bumped into the wall. Back into forward where he hit the table. Reverse again hitting the wall, forward again hitting the table. After rocking it back and forth like a teenager learning to parallel park, he managed to aim the Rascal in such a way that he ran over Mr. Leg Braces' toes and got out of the security area.

"You did that on purpose, you fake handicapped prick!"

The walkie-talkie crackled. "Hey Gary, will you bring me a hot dog when you come down? Gary? Gary?"

Best of all, Big Mike never had to buy a ticket.

27

IT HAS TO BE TOUGH to spend an entire day saying the same two words to people when you know they are going to have a violent reaction. Like a really bad case of eczema, you just get used to it.

"Fifty bucks," the parking attendant said.

A sample of some of the responses:

"You gotta be shitting me."

"No way."

"Cash? American?"

"There is no way I'm paying fifty bucks to park here. Okay, here you go."

"Is there valet?"

In a way, it became kind of a game to see which angry reaction people would come up with.

Then the armored vehicle pulled up. This was going to be the highlight of his day. It was some sort of army type truck, but it said Nassau County Police on the side. He knew what he should do, but he also knew what he was going to do.

"Fifty bucks."

"What?," said the officer in the driver's seat.

"Fifty bucks to park. Cash only."

"No, no, we're the police, we don't pay to park."

"Everybody pays to park."

"Look, on the side of the truck, it says Nassau County Police."

"What is this thing?"

"It's an MRAP. Mine resistant, bomb resistant, airtight, waterproof."

"What the hell do you need this for? Are people trying to bomb you while you're writing speeding tickets? How much does this thing cost?"

"About three hundred and fifty grand."

"So you're driving a three hundred and fifty thousand dollar bombproof car and you're trying to screw a working man out of fifty bucks? That ain't right."

"Now wait a minute, no one is trying to screw you out of anything. Normally, the police park for free."

"Listen, that may be how it goes in Nassau County, but that's not how it happens in New Jersey. If you don't pay to park, they take it out of my check. Which, let me tell you, ain't much."

"Okay, okay, we don't want you to get dinged on this deal."

He reached into his wallet and came up with twelve dollars.

"Hey guys, we gotta scrape up fifty bucks to park."

"I got ten."

"I got five."

"I got three."

"You have three dollars?"

"My wife took money out of my wallet."

"And if she hadn't taken money out of his wallet, he'd have four."

Slowly, but surely, they scraped together fifty bucks and handed it to the guy.

"Here you go, I'm glad we could make this right

for you."

"Thanks, man, I really appreciate it. Means a lot to me. You guys take care and write lots of tickets."

He shoved the fifty bucks in his pocket. Turning out to be a pretty good day so far.

Then things got really weird. A brown Chevy Cavalier pulled up. When the man rolled down the window it smelled like an industrial accident. The interior was completely melted. It looked like the world's ugliest chocolate fountain and it smelled like feet. There was only one thing to say.

"Fifty bucks."

"Fifty bucks?," said the guy with the eyepatch behind the wheel. "That's a lot."

He fished two tens and two fives out of his wallet, then peeled away the glovebox door like a piece of taffy. The Crock Pot pulled out the curled up, burnt owners manual, flipped open some pages and pulled out a twenty with the edges burned off. Good enough.

"What happened to your car, man?"

"Candle accident."

Mr. 176 and Ms. 191 parked without any drama except for having to pool their per diem money to cough up the fifty bucks. It seemed a little stiff at first, but this was, after all, a world class sporting event broadcast live on cable TV, so you have to expect the prices to be a little higher than normal. Putting on an outdoor bowling championship probably cost a pretty penny. The security costs alone must have been immense. They put their heads together on how to defeat what they figured to be an international incident level of security.

They stepped out of the vehicle and geared up. On the outside they appeared to be wearing normal black business suits, easier to blend in with the normal crowd. Except for today when the normal crowd was wearing very high-waisted slacks and baggy shirts with their names stitched onto them. Still, they had to work with what they had. Under the suits were matching Mac-10 submachine guns and Wisco-issued H&K pistols. Mr. 176 had a Kel-Tec .380 strapped to his ankle just in case and Ms. 191 had a serrated scuba diving knife as her back up weapon. Hanging from a shoulder strap she carried a five foot long plastic case while Mr. 176 set off his ensemble with an ugly looking black eye. Security might be tricky.

Stepping up to the security area they were immediately challenged by one of the staff.

"Do you have any beer in your possession?," asked the security guard, who was normally a part-time electrician.

"Did you say beer?," 191 asked.

"Yes, do you have any beer in your possession?"

"No, I do not have any beer in my possession."

"Okay, come on through."

She couldn't believe they made it. This seemed a little too easy.

"Hold on a second," another security guard said.

191 started to sweat, but she kept cool on the outside. Trust your training, she thought.

"What's in that case?"

Think fast, 191, think fast.

"It's a chair."

"You know we have chairs here at the

Meadowlands."

"Yes, but I like my chair."

"Suit yourself, have a nice day. Enjoy whatever it is they're doing here today."

Susie, Bernie and Leonard finally made it to the gate.

"Tickets, please."

"We don't need tickets, we're competitors."

"You didn't come in a limousine?"

"No, we came in a Dodge Neon," Bernie said.

"That was a joke."

"Sorry," Bernie said.

"Names."

"Fleischman and Steers."

"How do you spell that?"

"F-L-E-I..."

"No, the other one."

"S-T-E..."

"I'm just pulling your leg, buddy, I got you guys right here."

He checked them off the list and turned to Susie and said, "Ticket, please."

"Is that another joke? You're pretty funny."

"No joke, you need a ticket."

"But I'm with them. I'm his girlfriend."

Leonard froze. The world around him shifted into slow motion and looked like there was Vaseline around the edge of the lens. Had he heard that correctly? Did Susie say she was Leonard's girlfriend? The angels sang, he heard violins play, until she punched him in the arm.

"Tell her, Leonard."

"She's with me," Leonard stammered.

"Okay, but don't tell anybody I let you in without a ticket."

"Thanks."

"Hey, one more thing."

"Yes?"

"You're not trying to sneak in any beer are you?"

"Nope."

"Then you're good to go."

Ray Flanagan was having his usual luck. While forcing his fourth car off the expressway he bent the fender on his truck and it cut into his tire. He had to put on the spare and then use the baseball bat from under his seat to bend the damn fender back out. He finally got to New fucking Jersey and found the Meadowlands.

"Fifty bucks," the parking attendant said.

"To park in this dump? You should be paying me. I'm bringing up the value of this place."

"Fifty bucks, please."

"I'm one of the competitors, I'm sure we get free parking."

"No one gets free parking. I just got fifty bucks off a bunch of cops to park."

"No one gets free parking?"

"That's right. No one."

"I think you're going to give me free parking."

"I think you're wrong."

Ray grabbed the man's arm and pulled it inside the car. He reached up to the man's elbow with his other hand and popped the joint out of the socket.

"Hey man! Oww, that's my elbow."

Before he could get the word "elbow" out of his mouth Ray grabbed his other arm and repeated the process leaving the man stuck and helpless with his two arms hanging limp by his sides.

"Free parking?," Ray said. "Why I'd love free parking. Bye, bye. It won't hurt my feelings if you don't wave back."

That felt good. Ray was all warmed up for what he had to do next. He wasn't exactly sure what that would be, but he was ready to do whatever it would take to win. This was his one chance and he was going to make the most of it. And if people had to die, well, that's what they get for coming to New Jersey.

On the other side of the Meadowlands, in the VIP parking section, a long black limousine surrounded by New Jersey State Police motorcycles pulled into the lot. The official seal of the State of New Jersey on each door and state official New Jersey license plates on either end. As the limo pulled up to the parking lot attendant, the back window smoothly powered down revealing the smiling face of Governor Chris Christie. Always ready to take the opportunity to speak with a citizen, Governor Christie reached out one of his big hands and said, "Chris Christie, nice to meet you."

The parking attendant looked him straight in the eye and said, "Fifty bucks."

Welcome to New Jersey.

28

LEONARD AND BERNIE went into the locker room to prepare for their opening matches. Compared to the bathroom back at the bowling alley, this was a palace.

Their feet didn't even stick to the floor.

"Hey look, a whirlpool. We can use it between matches," Leonard said.

"Can you imagine the germs that are living in there?," Bernie said. "I can see the disease floating on the surface."

As they checked through their gear, a silver haired man entered the locker room. In a rich tenor voice he said, "What a dump. I'm used to being put up in a suite at the Wynn and here I am in a New Jersey locker room. With...who are you guys?"

"Bowlers," Bernie said.

"My career is crumbling right before my eyes."

It was Taylor Fenton, a boxing ring announcer who got famous after coining his famous catchphrase "It's Time To Tangle!"

"Hey, you're the 'It's Time To Tangle' guy," Leonard said.

"I have a name, you know, it's Taylor Fenton."

"I love that saying. We say it all the time before

league bowling night."

"That's fantastic, what's your name?"

"Leonard Fleischman."

"That's great Leonard, because what you're doing is a flagrant violation of the copyright I hold and vigorously defend regarding 'It's Time To Tangle' or 'ITTT' for short. You'll be hearing from my attorneys. A lot of them."

"So what are you doing here, Taylor?," Bernie asked, trying to brighten up the room a little.

"It's Mr. Fenton and what the fuck do you think I'm doing here? I'm gonna say 'It's Time To Tangle' before you cretins start bowling. They wanted me to say 'It's Time To Roll 'em' instead, but I told them if they want that they could go get some other guy. I say 'It's Time To Tangle' because that's my thing and I'm not changing it for anybody, you understand?"

"I see," said Bernie. "Anybody ever told you that you look a little like Donald Trump."

"You're the first and if you say that to me again, I'll have you killed. I know people."

"Well, it was great to meet you, too."

Fenton walked out just in time for Ray Flanagan to stagger in.

"Hello Leonard," Ray said. "Ready to get a major league, televised ass kicking today?"

"C'mon Ray," Leonard said, "some of the best bowlers in the world are here. There's real competition, pro quality stuff. What makes you think you're going to be handing out the ass kickings today?"

"Because I have to. You wouldn't understand."

"Like I wouldn't understand almost losing to a monkey?" Leonard shouldn't have said that, but he couldn't resist twisting the knife a little.

"Listen to me you sawed off son of a bitch," Ray started screaming. "That was against the rules, against the spirit of the game and one more ball I would have beaten that monkey anyway."

"Beating your monkey? In public?"

Ray started to go after Leonard, but a bunch of the other bowlers swarmed in and held Ray back.

"Hey, I'm just kidding, Ray," Leonard said, reaching out his right hand. "May the best man win."

"Fuck you, Leonard. I'm going to beat you, then kill you, then burn your body and then piss on the ashes."

"Okay, then."

Ray wheeled around to Bernie. "Do I know you?," he said.

"I don't think so, I'm Bernie Steers," he said, sticking out his right hand.

"I didn't say I wanted to know you, fuckface."

Ray dropped his gear in a locker and stomped off to the toilets. They could hear him coughing violently.

"He's not in a very good mood," Bernie said.

"I think Ray Flanagan is going to have a tough day," Leonard said.

That's when Taylor Fenton stormed back in.

"Did you idiots know about this?," the world famous announcer shouted in a very warm tone.

"Know about what, Mr. Fenton?"

"This!" He held up a flyer advertising the event. "I've introduced some of the greatest athletes the world has ever known. The best fighters of our age clamor to have me say their name. And now, in this New Jersey hell hole, I'm opening for a bowling monkey. Am I reading this right? Mr. Sprinkles, a primate, comes on right after me. This cannot stand. I'm calling my agent."

"I wonder if he still has that wig?," Bernie said. "I'd like to get that back."

The Meadowlands never looked better. The football field had been replaced with ten pairs of bowling lanes. All morning competitors had been bowling in the knockout rounds. As the field shrunk, workmen came in and removed the extra lanes until only two remained. These would be for the semi-finals and the finals, the matches that would make up the live taped television extravaganza being carried on many of your local cable systems coast-to-coast.

Ray slogged his way through the knockouts and, in the semi finals, he would face off against 15-year-old bowling phenom Annalisa Santina from Huntington Beach, California. With no formal training, just a natural gift, Annalisa had become the darling of the bowling world. If bowling tournaments could be won with Twitter votes and Facebook likes, Annalisa would walk away with the whole thing.

She'd become quite the ambassador for the bowling world appearing on Ellen, bowling in the middle of a Manhattan street on Jimmy Fallon, showing her signature tri-toned pastel shoes on the Wendy Williams shoe-cam. Annalisa even did the morning radio show with Ryan Seacrest.

"Annalisa," Ryan said, "how does it feel to be famous?"

"It's been really fun, people everywhere have been so nice."

"Have you gotten to ride around in limousines, people asking you for autographs? What's the most surprising thing about getting so famous so fast?"

"I was glad to get famous doing something I'm good at and something I'm proud of. At least it didn't happen like Kim Kardashian where I had to humiliate myself and then pretend I had some sort of talent."

"And let's go to break."

Bernie had played "clean" most of the way through the tournament, bowling with a traditional bowling ball and doing the best he could. Things got a little out of hand in the quarterfinals and Bernie fell behind. Badly.

It's not unusual for bowlers to use different balls in the course of a match. One ball may work better on one lane than the other. And as the match goes on, conditions change, oil patterns fluctuate and the ball reacts differently to the lane. No one gave it a single thought when Bernie picked up the flat blue ball.

Bernie needed a strike right now or he was done. And he'd need two more to get the win. He was bowling well, but the tournament and having his life threatened and witnessing a shootout was all starting to take its toll. Bernie didn't want to lose and he wasn't going to let that happen if he had a choice. Which he did.

He grabbed the ball and could feel the servos inside energize and come to life. As the ball's father he knew the default settings inside the ball were matched perfectly to his own swing. Since he wouldn't have time for any orientation throws, he'd have to guess. He sent the ball down the right side of the lane with a medium amount of spin, the ball hooked into the pocket for a very unremarkable shot, but all the pins went down. Bernie was back in the game.

His opponent matched with a strike and Bernie had to answer. He reached for the BX300.9 again. Did the ball learn enough the last time down the lane? Had the conditions changed? They were bowling outdoors after all. The ball was programmed to deal with temperature, lane conditions and spin, but it was never designed to compensate for wind, weather and God knows what was seeping out of the nearby swamp.

Bernie took five steps and threw the ball. Hard. It roared down the lane spinning furiously in a big arc hanging halfway over the gutter, then it caught and turned in aggressively, smashing through the pocket and sending the pins flying. A strike. With an exclamation point.

Game over and Bernie was moving on to the semis.

Against a guy named Leonard Fleischman.

Ray Flanagan watched intently on the monitor in the locker room. Bernie had switched balls and turned it around. Not uncommon, he'd done it himself. Sometimes a new ball performed better on the lane, sometimes it gave you a change in attitude, but there was something odd about that ball. Ray had heard rumors about a super secret bootleg bowling ball that could smoke anything else. A sort of high tech wonder with a bunch of computer crap inside. They said a cocker spaniel could strike with it. Ray had watched Bernie and, given the choice, Ray would take the cocker spaniel. And yet Bernie was killing. Was this the magic bowling ball hiding in plain sight?

At the front gate another man in a black suit showed up. Paid his fifty dollars to park, VIP ticket, no muss, no fuss, no one remembered him coming in. Mr. 221 was in the house.

29

WHEN YOU THINK of great sports match-ups throughout history you might think Ali versus Frazier, Cowboys versus 49ers, Nicklaus versus Watson. One match-up not appearing on the list is a mean old man with a nasty cough going head to head against a cute 15-year-old girl nicknamed "The Angel With A Hook of Gold." Still, it was the kind of match up the TV guys only dreamed about. And here it was.

Ray Flanagan played his part to the hilt. Hollywood couldn't have written him any better.

"I'm playing a little girl? Oh that's perfect. I've already had to beat a monkey and now I've got to go up against a girl," Ray said.

"Wait a minute," the reporter said, "are you comparing Annalisa to a monkey?"

"Not at all. They're totally different. She has better footwork, but the monkey threw a much stronger hook. On the other hand, he smelled terrible. I haven't smelled the girl yet."

The media went crazy with the story. And not in a good way.

Annalisa had never taken a lesson, she just seemed to pick up the game watching her Dad play. At age 8 she was regularly bowling 150 or more. Two years later she rolled her first perfect 300. Reporters immediately started calling her the Tiger Woods of bowling.

"I like bowling, but my mom says I can't join the tour until I pass Algebra II," she said.

Everyone was in love with Annalisa.

Except Ray.

The reporters tried their best to soften up his image, but Ray didn't make it any easier in his televised up close and personal segment.

"I understand you are wrestling with some very serious health issues right now," the reporter asked gently.

"Yeah."

"Tell us a little bit about that."

"Basically, my liver crapped the bed."

"Excuse me?"

"My liver is no good. It's solid as a rock, pickled from too many years of too much booze and if they don't find me a new one pretty quick I'm going to drop dead. With any luck, I'll keel over on TV. That would be pretty damn funny, you gotta admit."

"Are you bowling in this tournament to raise awareness for victims of liver disease?"

"Raising awareness? I don't give two shits about any of that. I just want to kick some ass and show people I can bowl. I could use a beer, you want one?"

Needless to say, America wasn't pulling for Ray Flanagan.

Annalisa came out to cheers, screams, handwritten signs (thoughtfully provided by the TV producers) and a blizzard of stuffed animals (also provided by those clever producers) being tossed onto the bowling lanes. She was an instant celebrity and the camera loved her. But to be a true hero you had to have a bad guy. The producers didn't need to provide one, they had Ray.

The bowling semi-finals turned into a Saturday night pro wrestling match as Ray stepped onto the lane to a chorus of boos.

"Go home, Ray!"

"Screw you, old man!"

"Bring back the monkey!"

This was a tough crowd and Ray loved it. After years on loading docks dealing with union toughs and lazy bosses, Ray's skin was thick as an old bomber jacket. Here, in godforsaken New Jersey, in front of thousands of people who wanted nothing more than to see him fail miserably, Ray Flanagan had finally found his place and his people. He could feel the hate and it gave him strength.

Annalisa wasn't just hype, she was the real thing. She could do things with a bowling ball that shouldn't be possible. Straight at the head pin, right in the pocket, Brooklyn side, splits of any combination. There wasn't a shot she couldn't make. Every strike, every pick up spare was greeted with thunderous applause. The crowd had found its hero.

Ray was not only an old guy, he was an old school power bowler. He drew the ball back way high above his head and threw it fast and hard. Every shot. Ray didn't have a finesse shot. In fact, he only had two shots. A high, hard shot that swept out in a wide arc hanging over the gutter and then cutting violently into the pocket. That was his strike shot. The other shot was his spare pick up ball, just a kindler, gentler version of the first shot. They weren't fancy, but they worked.

And they'd better work today.

Annalisa came out and started knocking down pins. Steady, reliable, textbook perfect form. When Ray looked up, he was ten pins down. Steady Ray, he thought. She's just a kid, let's see if she can take the heat.

The crowd had taken to screaming "In The Pocket!" on every shot Annalisa made. The trouble was they were screaming before she even released the ball, a clear infringement of the unwritten bowling code. The first time they cheered, she bowled a strike, but that was the last time it helped. The pressure was getting to her.

Every time Ray bowled they screamed, "Screw you, old man!" It really helped him find his center.

Annalisa left a pin, picked it up, then missed her target and left the ten pin. She plopped down in her chair and started to pout. The camera was close on her face as the first heartbreaking tear appeared and ran down her face.

Ray picked up his ball and sent an angry, spinning shot down the lane for a strike. Then one more, just to make sure his point was made loud and clear.

He pumped his fist in the air and was greeted by polite bowler applause. The Annalisa fans were already on their way to the concession stands.

Ray didn't care about those people, they weren't bowling fans five minutes ago, they wouldn't be bowling fans five minutes from now. His people were here and they knew what they had seen. A big, strong man beating a tenth grade girl.

It didn't sound so good when you put it that way.

"Leonard," Bernie said, "Let's talk."

"Let's."

"I'm gonna do everything I can to beat you."

"Everything?"

"Well, not everything."

"What are you talking about, Bernie?"

"The ball."

"The magic bowling ball?"

"Yes. I've already used it a couple of times. It knows the lanes, it's ready to roll."

"That's a decision you have to make. You're virtually unbeatable with that ball."

"I know, but I promise, I'm not rolling it. We'll play mano a mano."

Bernie stuck out his right hand, Leonard took it.

"You're a good man, Leonard Fleischman. You be good to my daughter or I'll kill you." Bernie smiled as fathers always do while issuing that line. Said in jest, but not completely.

"Get away from my husband, you kidnapper!," screamed a woman from the other side of the locker room.

Lorraine Steers were standing across the locker room. She was staring down the very short barrel of the Colt Detective Special.

"Wait, I didn't kidnap anyone," said Leonard.

Lorraine fired. Fortunately for Leonard, the Detective Special was notoriously inaccurate and the shot went high and poked a hole in the whirlpool tub.

"Hold on, I can explain."

The next round went wide and lodged in a leftover Joe Namath bobblehead.

"Lorraine, stop shooting, it's okay," Bernie said.

"This is Susie's boyfriend."

"Susie has a boyfriend?"

"I'm Leonard Fleischmann, Mrs. Steers. Nice to meet you."

"He seems nice. Sorry about almost shooting you."

"It's not the first time."

"How did you find me?," Bernie asked.

"I tracked your phone, just like on CSI. I was worried about you."

"Pretty impressive detective work."

"Why didn't you tell me, Bernie?"

"I don't know. I'm sorry. I guess I felt like I had to do this on my own."

"And it's good thing, Mrs. Steers," Leonard added. "Because you would have been in a lot of danger. We almost got killed."

"Bernie, what happened?"

"Chased by killers, hit men and the Wisco Security Team."

"They're real?"

"Yes, but, Lorraine, you shouldn't be here."

"In New Jersey?"

"No, the locker room, it's the men's locker room. And where'd you get that gun?"

"From my father. He gave it to me. In case I needed to shoot you."

"Okay, I'll just leave you two alone," Leonard said and went into the back section of the locker room to take a leak.

He never saw the man in the black suit.

Mr. 221 grabbed Leonard by the neck with a pair

of bowling shoestrings. He pulled back hard bringing Leonard's ear close to his mouth.

"You're a good bowler, Fleischman. Just the wrong guy at the wrong time," 221 hissed.

Leonard struggled hard, but he was running out of air. He managed to get his feet up on a sink and pushed back hard driving the man into the wall. The strangler was big, strong and was holding on to the right end of the string. He collected himself, gave another tug on Leonard's throat and continued.

"Bernie Steers is my kid brother. He hasn't seen his big brother Barney in 30 years. He thinks I'm dead, but I'm back to make his dreams come true. Now die already, Fleischman, I've got things to do."

Leonard responded by turning from blue to purple.

There was a loud clank, a shot rang out, the room filled with blue smoke and the big man in the black suit shuddered and slowly sank to the floor.

As the blood came back into Leonard's head, he was having a hard time believing what he was seeing. His Uncle Arnie standing in a bathroom stall with the door open, his pants around his ankles and a smoking flintlock pistol in his hand.

"Is that a flintlock?," Leonard asked.

"That's right. Carried one of these in the War of 1812."

"You fought in the War of 1812?"

"You're damn right I did, we sent those German bastards packing."

"Uncle Arnie, I don't think the Germans, never mind. Pull your pants up and let's get out of here."

With Annalisa out of the picture, the bowling crowd had thinned out a bit waiting for the final match. Bernie or Leonard, they didn't seem to care much who won. The media didn't seem to care, either. There was no behind the scenes story showing old photos of Bernie with long hair and a beard standing at his drafting table at Wisco headquarters. No inside access shots of Leonard running the show at Massapequa Pin and Pub. Although two mass shootings at the same bowling alley may have scared off the camera crew.

It was just Bernie and Leonard standing by the ball return, looking down at a few close friends and family. Leonard could see Susie right up front, Jim Steele hitting on a woman old enough to be his mother and Uncle Arnie wandering off toward a nacho stand.

"We fought for this country's freedom," Uncle Arnie would say, "so we could enjoy the truly American things we love. Like hot dogs and nachos and reality television."

It was a heartwarming scene.

The pair warmed up, threw a few balls and then it was game on.

Leonard had seen Bernie bowl before. Classic 1970's technique. Four step approach, big swing, hard pose at the finish. He was good, but certainly could be better if he'd move up a few decades. And while he had time-honored technique, he didn't have that gift certain bowlers have. Call it luck, call it strength, call it what you will, but any bowler can make the pins go down when they throw a perfect ball, it's when that ball is an inch or two off target that bad things happen.

And bad things were happening to Bernie Steers.

With two temporary lanes elevated above a crowd at a football stadium, the conditions were driving Bernie crazy. There was wind to consider, the moving sun to deal with. Bernie was used to bowling in controlled conditions where he controlled the conditions. He tried to visualize being back in the testing basement at Wisco, but he couldn't do it.

Just as Bernie was throwing the ball to start the fourth frame, a drunk slurred out "In The Pocket!" causing Bernie to split. He picked it up, but it was the beginning of the end of his game.

Leonard was nothing if not consistent. This wasn't his best game, but it certainly wasn't his worst. He was bowling plenty good enough to take Bernie.

Twelve pins down, Bernie needed a miracle to pull this out. There was one waiting. Leonard was sitting in the chair looking down at his shoes and concentrating hard, he'd never notice if Bernie made the switch. Two throws with the magic ball and he was back in this match. Leonard was younger and stronger, using the BX300.9 would be an equalizer, he justified. He opened his right hand over the air dryer and moved it to the ball return, his hand hovered over the flat blue orb that could save his game.

Then he made a critical error.

He looked down. And saw Susie looking up at him.

Bernie thought of the long nights in the lab. The times he'd stayed at the office for days on end because he was close to a breakthrough. The birthdays, the recitals, the skinned knees – he'd missed them all because he was at work developing the magical ball that was now just inches from his hand. The ball that would make his bowling dreams come true. He hadn't been there for Susie or Lorraine, but maybe he could be there for them now.

He picked up his regular ball and let it rip. It slipped a little as he threw it and never looked good going down the lane, but somehow, some way, all the pins fell. An ugly strike to be sure, but a strike nonetheless.

Ten pins. Brooklyn side.

Leonard answered with a strike of his own and then a spare.

Bernie still had a chance. He took four steps, swept the ball back as far as he could and powered the ball down the lane with everything he had. It wasn't enough, he left two pins.

Bernie picked up the spare and managed to close up the score to a respectable margin, but he didn't have enough to beat Leonard. It was a great game. And an honest one.

"Good game, Bernie. And thanks."

"Thanks. Good game yourself."

As they stepped off the alley, Leonard turned to Bernie and said, "I met your brother."

"My brother? What the hell are you talking about? My brother's been dead for 30 years. You just beat me and now you want to rub my face in it?"

Bernie started to stomp away, Leonard grabbed his arm and turned him around.

"Look at my neck."

Bernie slid his glasses down his nose and peered at the bright red bruise around Leonard's neck.

"He grabbed me from behind, tried to strangle me and claimed to be your brother. Big guy, little older than you. Said his name was Barney."

Bernie was astonished.

"Where is he now?"

"Dead. In the bathroom area inside the locker room."

Bernie started running for the locker room. Leonard and Susie were right behind him. When they got to the locker room they were shocked by what they saw. Or what they didn't see.

"He was right here, I swear," Leonard said.

"There's no body, no crime scene tape," Bernie said. "I watch TV, I know what happens after a murder."

"There isn't even any blood," Susie said.

"Then who strangled me? And who did Uncle Arnie shoot?"

30

THE FINALS WERE SET and the TV guys were in a deep funk about it.

It would be the grumpy geezer who whipped America's Sweetheart versus a chubby Jewish guy who worked in a bowling alley. They could hear people coast to coast switching over to a Judy Judge rerun.

What they didn't realize is they were about to broadcast the sports show of the century. All the players were taking their positions.

Mr. 176 and Ms. 191 were charged with getting their hands on the BX300.9 and, if possible, Bernie Steers. They wanted the ball in one piece, they weren't so particular about Bernie. Then there was revenge to think about. Wisco Security Special Agents were supposed to be above petty emotions like pain and retribution, but when it was one of their own, things were different. Mr. 221 was dead and they didn't know why or how. They had cleared the scene of evidence, but they knew one of these bowlers killed their boss, they just didn't know who. Which meant they had the green light for collateral damage.

Big Mike, aboard the best-armed Rascal scooter in the history of Medicare fraud mobility devices, was committed to taking out Leonard. The scooter gave him unfettered access to the field. No one ever challenged a cripple.

The Crock Pot knew he was supposed to kill Leonard, but after watching him bowl, he started to have second thoughts. If I kill him, Crock Pot thought, he won't be able to give me lessons. Life was filled with tough choices.

Nassau County Police Detective Tommy Hanrahan had tailed the big guy in the black suit to the Meadowlands. He wasn't sure what was going on, but he was going to do something about it. Maybe. If not, he'd do what he always did, watch a little bowling and have a few pops at the bar.

The Nassau County police department was in full riot gear and way out of their jurisdiction. The organizers were happy to see them. Even happier because they didn't have to pay them.

Susie was here to get her Dad back.

Leonard was here to start a new chapter.

And Taylor Fenton was here to make a paycheck.

"Christ on a cracker," Fenton said. "This is what I'm supposed to announce? I wouldn't book this lineup to open a landfill."

The TV camera lights came on and Fenton dutifully straightened his cummerbund and snapped into character. He hated being here, he hated this sport, he hated the opening ceremonies, but it beat having an actual job.

"This is celebrity sports announcer Taylor Fenton, welcoming you to the First Annual Jani-San 100 Grand Bowling Invitational, presented by Scratch-Eze Antifungal Spray. The winner gets a cool one hundred thousand dollars and the opportunity to compete on the pro bowling tour. It's going to be exciting stuff, so stay tuned. But first, please stand for our national anthem performed by the surviving members of the Lawrence Welk Orchestra."

While the band was using a chorus of accordions to ruin the Star Spangled Banner, Ray and Leonard got ready to go.

"Ray, I just wanted to wish you good luck," said Leonard extending his right hand.

"I hope you fuck the whole thing up," Ray answered. "Let's be honest here. I'm an old man. I'm dying. I have nothing to lose. I'm going to go out there and make you my bitch."

"I hope you can throw the ball as well as you can work your mouth."

"You've seen me bowl, you know I've got it. You know I can beat you."

"We're about to find out. How's your liver holding up?"

"Just fine," Ray said. He reached into his bowling bag, pulled out two airline bottles of Crown Royal, opened them both, put them in his mouth at the same time and drained them. "And now, my liver is feeling even better."

Ray started to cough violently which Leonard took as a sign the conversation was over.

"Thank you Lawrence Welk Orchestra," said Taylor Fenton. "That was a wunnerful, wunnerful." He couldn't believe he was reading this crap. He was happy he had insisted on a bank wire transfer in advance, the appearance money already snug in his account in the Caymans.

"Next up, the bowling sensation that is sweeping the country. I'm told this little fella actually entered a tournament and came one shot away from beating one of the men who is in the final round. Let's give a warm, New Jersey welcome to Sprinkles Morgenstern, the bowling chimp who almost beat Ray Flanagan!"

Leonard just saw a blur out of the corner of his eye as Ray ran from the locker room. He was pretty thick-skinned, but he hadn't quite gotten over almost being beaten by a monkey.

Sprinkles strutted onto the lanes like he owned the place, which, like any good performer, he did. Resplendent in his bowling shirt, matching bowling shoes and platinum blonde Farrah Fawcett wig, Sprinkles was working it.

"I've got to admit, the wig looks better on him than it did on me," Bernie said.

"Let's just leave that alone, Dad."

The monkey picked up a ball and threw the awesome spin he was famous for. The ball swung out wide and crushed the pins for a strike. The crowd went wild. Sprinkles jumped up on the ball return and screamed his approval. This time he picked up two balls and threw them at the same time. The balls crossed mid-alley and crushed the pins again. Another strike, another roar from the crowd.

By now Ray had made it to the edge of the stage. He stooped over, caught his breath, hawked up a bloody lunger and went after Sprinkles. Ray ran for the chimp at full speed and the crowd went completely nuts thinking this was part of the act.

Taylor Fenton improvised. "It's Ray Flanagan, the man who was almost beat by the monkey, here to get his revenge. Get 'em, Ray!"

The chimp jumped on and off the ball return, up and down off chairs, into the tournament director's lap and back out again, cleverly evading Ray at every turn. The producers were cheering up. Even they had to admit it was pretty good television.

"Camera 2, stay on the monkey!," the director screamed.

Finally, Sprinkles had enough. He jumped onto Ray's head, bit him on the face and scampered into the crowd bouncing off people's shoulders as he went using his free hand to hold the wig on his head.

"That looks like it's really gotta hurt," deadpanned Fenton.

Wrestling crowds are used to seeing fake blood all over the place and that's what they figured they were seeing this time as Ray held his hand to the side of his bleeding face.

"You had it coming!," the crowd taunted.

"PETA! PETA! PETA!"

"Camera 3," the director screamed. "Get as close as you can. Blood! Blood will get us on SportsCenter for sure!"

Ray made it back down to the locker room where it was revealed that the monkey bite was very real.

"When was the last time you had a tetanus shot?," the first aid woman asked.

"1975."

"You should probably have this looked at by, you know, a doctor or something."

"Just patch it up, I've got bowling to do."

Leonard looked on in horror as they used super glue to seal up some of the cuts and gauze to cover the rest. The right side of his head was still wrapped with a pus-covered bandage where his ear used to be, now his left cheek was covered in gauze and medical tape. It would be like bowling against the mummy.

This guy was nuts. And Leonard would get to stand right next to him in a few minutes. Perfect.

Ms. 191 had been watching the whole ridiculous scene keeping her eye on one thing and one thing only. The flat blue ball Bernie left in the ball return. It would soon be right where it belonged.

31

"LADIES AND GENTLEMEN, your attention, please," boomed professional boxing ring announcer slumming for a paycheck, Taylor Fenton.

No more monkeys, no more accordions, he could finally get to the kind of work he was trained for, saying people's names, how big they were and where they were from.

"Standing a commanding six feet four inches and hailing from South Farmingdale, New York, you met him before with Mr. Sprinkles the bowling chimp, please welcome the Lumberjack of the Lanes..."

Lumberjack of the Lanes?, Ray thought. What the hell is this idiot talking about?

Fenton thought that was a pretty good nickname considering he'd made it up on the spot.

"...Raaaaayyyyyyyy Flanagan."

A lukewarm response from the crowd. Except for the boos.

"Sprinkles! Sprinkles! Sprinkles!," went the new chant.

Ray wasn't looking too good for his first live TV appearance. The left half of his face was covered with pretty much everything in the first aid kit and the right side of his head had a droopy bandage that was yellow with wound drainage. It was even more disgusting in HD.

"Stretching the tape at five feet six and one half inches..."

That's what Leonard got for letting Uncle Arnie fill out the entry form.

"...From Massapequa, Long Island, club pro and host of the best birthday parties in Nassau County, it's the Beast of the Boards, the Mench of Massapequa, Leeeoooonnnnaarrrddd Fleeiiiissscchhhmmmaannn!"

Another tepid round of applause.

If you weren't America's bowling sweetheart or a monkey, there was no pleasing this crowd.

They threw a few warm up balls and then got right to it. Both were seasoned league bowlers and knew what to do. The first few frames were close. Matching strike for strike and spare for spare, no one giving an inch. Even the announcers, who had to be taught what "strike" and "spare" meant minutes before the broadcast, were impressed.

"They are neck and neck, Jim," announcer number one said.

"Pretty impressive stuff, Bob," announcer number two added in the way of in-depth analysis.

As the game wore on, Ray started to wear down. His liver was failing and his kidneys were about to join in. His skin was waxy, his eyes were yellow, he smelled like he was sweating cheap whiskey and things were starting to get a little foggy. The side of his head, where his ear used to be, was itching like crazy, but he couldn't scratch it because that would start the bleeding again. He wasn't sure what the PBA rule was on this, but bleeding profusely on the lane might result in a forfeit. And the other side of his face hurt bad. As soon as this was over he was going to find that monkey and barbecue his hairy little ass.

Still, Ray was hanging in there, but falling a little farther behind with every frame. He was eight pins down and running out of time. Leonard was working on a spare. He stepped up to his approach, focused on his goal and threw it hard. Strike.

Fuck, Ray thought.

Leonard followed with another strike. He had Ray on the ropes, but he knew Ray was a tough guy to kill off.

Ray needed something. More than something, he needed a miracle. That's when the bowling gods decided to smile on Ray Flanagan. They had taken his wife, they had taken his liver, they had taken his ear and part of his face, but now they were about to repay those debts and then some. The flat blue ball hiding right there in plain sight. Just sitting in the ball return, waiting for Ray to use it. Practically begging for Ray to use it.

He hesitated. Ray thought about the guys at work, his old Army buddies, the poor sap whose hand he crushed to get into the tournament. Then he thought, ah fuck those guys, and picked up the ball. Was he crazy or did the ball shake a little when he picked it up, like it was turning on or something? He got the feel of it and, even though the holes were drilled a little close together for him, he could make it work.

Ray shortened up his approach, stepped up to the line and threw what, for him, was a pretty easy shot. The ball started off line, bad shot, Ray thought, disaster. Then it seemed to find its way. The ball rolled out to the edge, seemed to actually begin spinning faster and then cut straight into the pocket for a strike.

No one was more amazed than Ray.

Except for Ms. 191.

And no one was more pissed than Bernie.

"Did you see that? He used my ball," Bernie said to Susie. "He used my goddamn ball. I'm filing a formal complaint."

"With who?," Susie said. "The janitor? It's an unsanctioned event. They had a bowling monkey for Christ's sake."

Ray threw the magic ball again, this time with a renewed sense of energy. Hard in the pocket for an angry strike.

"We are all tied up, Jim," said bowling announcer one.

"Looks like it's shaping up to be a really close match, Bob," said bowling announcer two.

"Let's go to the tenth."

"That's the last one, Bob, so it's really the last chance for one of these guys to win."

"Right you are, Jim."

Leonard had been in tough spots before, but he knew what to do. He was completely focused and barely noticed anything going on around him. Just the ball, the pins and nothing else. He picked up his ball and threw it hard with a big, impressive hook designed to intimidate the opponent. The ball swung way out, hooked in and hit home. Strike.

In Leonard's opinion, ball number two was the key to the tenth frame. You didn't have the adrenaline like the first ball and you didn't have the pressure like the third. He relied on this training and his technique. Five steps, smooth arm swing, big finish. Less colorful than the last throw, but the same result. Strike.

The crowd started to murmur. They didn't really know what was happening, but they knew it was something.

"Something really special is happening here, Jim," said announcer one.

"Sure seems like it, Bob," said announcer two.

The third ball was the clutch shot, so Leonard didn't think about it, he just went up and threw it. Bad move, he missed the pocket by two inches and left the ten pin standing. Rookie mistake, but maybe it would be good enough to win. Ray would have to throw three strikes in a row to win it.

Ray loved being the underdog.

The underdog with a secret weapon.

32

THREE BALLS, THREE STRIKES. That's all Ray needed. To get his life back on track. To prove everyone wrong. To get a new liver. The way he understood it, new livers were pretty much automatic for sports heroes, which he was on the verge of becoming. He hoped his wife was watching and that she would see the error of her ways. (She wasn't and she didn't.)

The first throw with the magic ball was just that, magic. He started it outside, hung it right over the edge and then watched the ball turn like it had eyes. Straight in for a strike.

Ray was a good bowler, but anyone could throw one strike. Throwing three in a row was a different story altogether.

The monkey bite was really starting to ache now and blood was starting to seep through the Frankenbandage cobbled together from the first aid kit. Ray was feeling a little woozy. Might be the first symptoms of rabies, he thought.

He picked up the blue ball and did what he always did. Four steps and a swing. Another textbook strike.

The crowd figured out this whole thing was coming down to the last ball. Strike or go home a loser. Even the announcers caught on.

"Jim, if he strikes here he wins the whole thing," announcer number one said.

"That's right, Bob," announcer number two said.

"Bet he's under a lot of pressure."

"And he's bleeding like a hemophiliac at a knife throwing convention."

"Can't believe you said that, Jim."

"Just trying to add a little color for the folks at home. And the color of the day is red."

"Disgusting, Bob."

This was it and Ray knew it. Sure he had cheated, but life had cheated him and today was the day all accounts were settled.

There was nothing Leonard could do. He'd rolled the best game he could, now he just sat there like a passenger in a car that was out of control. Hunched over with his elbows on his knees afraid to watch, but also afraid to miss it. He froze.

Which is exactly what Big Mike was waiting for.

From the floorboard of the Rascal, Big Mike pulled out an AR-15 with a folding stock. He took aim and started squeezing the trigger on the easiest shot in his life. Who would even suspect the guy in the scooter? He'd roll out of the Meadowlands without a word.

The Crock Pot caught the glint of the AR-15's scope out of the corner of his good eye. Just a hit man's instinct, he figured. That's when he made up his mind. He grabbed a ball off the Pinknockerz display stand (he was a Wisco man himself, but in a pinch this would do) and he rolled hard toward Big Mike. The ball skidded like crazy on the astroturf and didn't break the way the Crock Pot had intended.

Instead, it hit a woman's foot, cracking four out of five metatarsal bones, hopped up in the air and came down right on Mike's broken pinkie toe.

Flinching from the pain caused Mike to jerk the rifle as he pulled the trigger sending the bullet high, just over Leonard's head. Leonard hardly noticed, because Ray had started the downswing on the shot that would seal the deal.

Mike dropped the gun and grabbed for his foot bumping into the control lever sending the Rascal screaming in reverse at top speed dragging his shattered toe on the ground. He flailed at the controls getting his hands on the power switch a split second too late to keep him from slamming into the Nassau County Police Department MRAP parked on the sideline.

An IED, or improvised explosive device, is a weapon commonly used by terrorists to attack troops. IEDs come in all shapes and sizes, but no one could recall seeing one built into the chassis of a Rascal scooter crammed with hundreds of rounds of live ammunition. The MRAP vehicle was designed to defend soldiers from exactly this type of weapon, which the fine men in blue from Nassau County had the opportunity to field test that day in the Meadowlands.

Since the Rascal was already jammed underneath the MRAP when the explosion started, the force had nowhere to go, but up. The gift from the citizens of Nassau County was blown ten feet straight up in the air tearing both the front and rear axles completely off the vehicle. The officers inside were well protected. The same couldn't be said for the tax dollars of Nassau County.

The magic ball had just left Ray's hand on its way to securing his bowling destiny. Ms. 191 was about to send it somewhere else.

Hidden in a tunnel in the closed upper deck of the Meadowlands was 191, her long plastic case open next to her, the contents now resting on her shoulder. A military issue fly-by-wire anti-tank missile. You pull the trigger, keep your eye on the target and let the computers do the rest. She would end the magic ball right here, right now.

Mr. 176 had her six covered so she could focus on setting up the shot.

"Hold it right there, you're under arrest," said Tommy Hanrahan, a little shaky for two reasons. Number one, he had been drinking beer instead of liquor all day. It was a shock to the system. And two, he was totally winded from climbing the stairs to the upper deck. They turned off the elevators to save electricity. Cheap bastards, Tommy thought.

Hanrahan caught the pair red-handed and he was covering the big guy with his service revolver. He'd drag them down to headquarters and make them tell the truth. Then it was pension time.

176 looked over to 191 who gave him an almost imperceptible nod. He turned to Hanrahan and casually punched him in the nose sending him staggering backward. He easily relieved Tommy of his revolver and slipped it into his pocket.

"Why don't you go be a good policeman and let us get our work done."

She pulled the trigger.

With a loud whoosh, the missile flew down to meet the pins right as the magic ball hooked into the pocket.

The man in the custom windowpane suit with the baby blue fedora nestled atop a wondrous pile of dreadlocks would have stuck out anywhere, but it was especially acute standing among thousands of pasty, middle aged bowlers. Even so, no one noticed as Franklin Roosevelt slipped a small black box from his jacket pocket. As the magic ball was about to reach the pins, he thumbed the box's single button. A red one.

Terrorism experts have worked for years to find ways to keep people safe during explosions. Exactly zero of them have worked on a scenario involving a crowd attending an outdoor bowling event in a football stadium. Leonard and Ray were blown off the lane as the wooden boards turned into splinters. Fragments of bowling pins pelted the crowd causing several dozen minor injuries that would require explaining to Blue Cross over and over how it happened. The windows in the press box shattered, one goal post blew over and, in a truly heartbreaking development, the nachos cart was upended sending a gallon of golden cheese-like substance spreading out on the concrete floor.

"That was an exciting end to a pretty impressive day, Bob."

"I never knew bowling could be so explosive, Jim."
"Good one, Bob."

Hearing the blast from inside the stadium, Jimmy and Timmy begged the parking attendant to let them in.
"Fifty bucks," he said.
"I told you we don't have fifty bucks, hell, my pants are taped together."

33

SINCE LEONARD WAS AHEAD at the time of the explosion, he was declared the winner and awarded the one hundred thousand dollar prize and the one year spot on the PBA Tour. When he's not bowling at a luxurious pro event like the Greater Cleveland Open, he and Susie bowl Thursday league nights.

Jimmy and Timmy Duval spent months trying, unsuccessfully, to collect expense money from Dale Saxby. Their other client, Mr. 221, won't return their calls. They've decided to move forward with their newest plan to kidnap and ransom 1980's pop star Rick Springfield. They figure he's worth a cool $7,500.

Mr. 176 and Ms. 191 were awarded the Star of the Lane, the highest honor given by the Wisco Corporation. In accordance with Wisco Security rules, they were given the awards in secret and must never tell a soul. The actual medals were collected after the brief ceremony and returned to the company safe.

Despite his continued drinking, predilection toward violent behavior and other risk factors, Ray

Flanagan received a new liver. He quit bowling and now plays competitive Jenga.

Bernie Steers never went back to Waukesha, Wisconsin. He liked New Jersey so much that he and Lorraine bought a convenience store in Montclair. He still tinkers in the garage and is almost done with the BX300.10.

Little Sally, aka the Crock Pot, left New Jersey a hero after using a bowling ball to thwart a terrorist attack. He was named an honorary member of the Pinknockerz Pro Bowling Team and was interviewed for Bowler's World magazine. His friends call him One Ball. He's learned to live with it.

Uncle Sally led a successful fundraising campaign to buy the Nassau Police Department a new armored personnel carrier. He sold his interest in Massapequa Pin and Pub and now owns a chain of spectacularly unsuccessful video rental stores.

Big Mike's remains were identified from a partial serial number found on a piece of a stainless steel orthopedic plate discovered in the debris. Big Mike's mother sued the manufacturer of the Rascal scooter and settled out of court for $1.6 million.

Uncle Arnie is still Leonard's manager and enjoys watching Judge Judy, although he's been dabbling with Judge Joe Brown.

Dale Saxby, CEO of Jani-San, thought he had a really solid Plan B. He figured he would present one of those giant checks for one hundred thousand dollars and then just never send the real check. Who knew Bank of America would actually accept a giant check? He recently sent his son to start their new office, Jani-San of Fallujah.

Tommy Hanrahan received a Purple Heart for the broken nose he sustained while, according to his own detailed report, he was giving mouth-to-mouth to a nun.

Franklin Roosevelt was offered the job to lead the Wisco Security Team for twice his Pinknockerz salary. He turned it down when they rejected his demand for a lavish clothing allowance.

Sprinkles Morgenstern was given his own show, "It's Sprinkles!," Thursday nights at 8 pm on NBC.

34

SERIOUS LEAGUE BOWLERS would never want to admit this, but America's bowling alleys would be out of business if every Saturday and Sunday hordes of kids didn't get dropped off by their parents so they can eat horrible sheet cakes and exchange Lego sets. The kids drink Pepsi by the pitcher and participate in the one sport that every bowler hates with a white-hot passion: bumper bowling.

The everyone-gets-a-trophy version of bowling, bumper bowling involves placing huge squishy pads in the gutters of the lanes. Instead of the character building experience of watching a ball clunk into the gutter and ever so slowly roll down to the end resulting in a score of zero, the bumpers happily bounce the ball back into the lane virtually guaranteeing little Johnny hits at least a few pins and feels really good about himself.

Yay.

They're like bowling training wheels. Complete with the false self-esteem package.

Little Frances Steinberg's tenth birthday party at the Bergen County Bowling Barn ("Bergen County Bowling Barn is fun for the whole family. Ask about our Happy Hour drink specials.") was a pretty typical affair of fifteen nine- and ten-year-olds, a quarter sheet cake with a picture of some indiscriminate boy band plastered on it, festive paper tablecloths on rickety folding tables and, of course, the sport of kings, bumper bowling.

"Good try, Ashley!," the moms cried.

"Use both hands if you have to," the dads advised. "It's okay."

"Keep your hands to yourself, Jimmy!"

The future of bowling starts here. God help us.

The kids were issued smelly rental shoes, selected balls in their favorite color and the computer dutifully kept score.

Ashley, with the pink ball, rolled a 28.

Nicky, with the black ball, rolled a 53.

Christina, with the sparkly green ball, rolled a 44.

And ten-year-old Frankie Ferragamo, with the plain blue ball, the veteran of the group since he was bowling for the third time, rolled a very respectable 206.

In the sub-sub basement of the Wisco Bowling Corporation, the team scrambled.

ABOUT THE AUTHOR

VINNY MINCHILLO has done a lot of things sensible people don't do. He's an advertising creative director and contributed to the best-selling *Worst Case Scenario Survival Handbook*. Vinny's raced lawnmowers, demo derby cars and was a winner on *Wheel of Fortune*. He lives in Plano, Texas with his wife in a home filled with spoiled pets and vintage typewriters.

20523131R00143

Made in the USA
Middletown, DE
29 May 2015